"When are we going to Nassau to get Erikson out of that jail?" asked Hazel.

Hazel is my girl friend, all redheaded six feet of her. And she knew everything about me. Everything.

"When are we WHAT?" I said it so vehemently I blew a shower of sparks from my cigarette. We both batted at them furiously to keep the bed from catching fire. "What the hell did you say?"

"You know you can't leave him there," Hazel said calmly. "If you can't get anyone in Washington to act, that leaves you. . . ." Then she added softly, "And I won't have you running out on me. We're going together."

OPERATION BREAKTHROUGH

Dan J. Marlowe

A FAWCETT GOLD MEDAL BOOK

Fawcett Publications, Inc. / Greenwich, Conn.

OPERATION BREAKTHROUGH

ONE

THE BANK was on the ground floor of a four-story downtown Nassau office building. My watch said ten minutes past midnight when we started up the rust-encrusted fire escape at the rear of the department store next to the bank. I could feel the perspiration breaking out on the back of my neck in the humidity of the Bahamian night as we lugged our equipment up to the roof. With anyone less strong than Karl Erikson for a pack-horse partner it would have taken more than one trip.

The building was on Shirley Street, a block away from Barclay's, Sassoon's, Chase Manhattan, and the other large banks on Bay Street in the financial district. This bank advertised a complete trust and investment service. We were interested in neither.

I paused for a breather on the roof. At that height the cool shore breeze was both noticeable and welcome. The scars from my plastic surgery itch when I perspire, especially under my wig. During the next few hours I was due to itch a good deal, and I didn't mind postponing it momentarily.

When Karl Erikson placed one of his rare phone calls to Washington just before sunset that evening and began talking about changes in a banana shipment, I guessed even before he came away from the telephone that something had gone off the rails. His guarded conversation translated into the fact that we had to move the operation up twenty-four hours because what we were after inside the bank might not be there the next day.

It put a definite squeeze on my carefully timed plan. For one thing, we wouldn't be able to get clear of the island immediately after we completed the job. The getaway arrangements set up by Erikson involved a lot of governmental red tape, and the system was too rigid to react to sudden changes. So now we were committed to playing cat-and-mouse with the British-trained Bahamian police force for a day and a night until the prearranged transportation showed up. I didn't like it, but there was nothing I could do about it.

The department store roof was high enough so I could see, against the blackness of the night, a portion of the crescent of pink sand beach near the tourist hotels. Muted phosphoresence sequined the small wavelets lapping the shore. There was almost no surf. The air around us was heavy with the fragrance of frangipani and mimosa growing in every open space and in the numerous window boxes in front of the stores in the Bay Street business district.

"What's the hangup, Earl?" Erikson demanded impatiently. He kept his voice down. Sound travels widely in the tropical night.

"Nothing," I said. "Let's move to the other roof."

We were wearing dark business suits and dress shoes. Erikson had suggested black coveralls and tennis shoes, but I pointed out that two men so attired would have difficulty blending into the local scenery if anything went wrong.

Erikson scooped up the heavier of our two canvas bags and walked to the roof edge I had marked on our diagram. He made it look easy as he leaped across the intervening space to the next building. I picked up the other bag and set my teeth as I confronted the eight-foot space with a litter-filled alley below. I'm not fond of heights, but I backed off, took a run at it, and jumped without giving myself time to think.

I jumped too far, of course, skidded, then righted myself. The bank building was closed after nine in the evening, and no watchman was on duty except on the ground floor premises the bank occupied. There were several alarms scattered throughout the building, a system sophisticated enough to insure that even a good technician would be almost sure to trigger an alarm at some point during his trespassing.

When I first studied the wiring diagrams webbing the building, I thought we might have to import an expert to knock out the alarm system. Then I studied the schematic further and realized it wouldn't be necessary. The alarms were a handicap only if they kept us from getting into the vault and escaping afterward. The more I studied the circuits, the more sure I became that it was going to take more than flashing lights or ringing bells to stop us.

I'd obtained the wiring diagrams of the bank our first night in Nassau by burglarizing the blueprint room in the office of the bank's architect. Erikson carried a portable copier, and we made duplicates of the bank plans. I was pleased to find that the architect was the meticulous type who made notes and amplified drawings on the original prints of all bank reconstruction, even of the cosmetic face-lifting kind.

A door led down from the roof into the interior of the building. I checked it automatically, but it was locked as I expected. My penlight disclosed the tiny, silvered wires of the alarm system. I turned to the small adjoining structure housing the mechanism for the building's elevators. The prints indicated it was neither locked nor bugged, and it represented the one major weakness I had found in the bank's security arrangements.

Karl Erikson crowded inside behind me when I tugged open the door gently and entered the small building. I reached inside my jacket, dug under the chamois holster containing a compact Smith & Wesson .38 special, and removed a screwdriver from the multipocketed vest I was wearing. Four salt-corroded screws on a section of the elevator shaft's tin roof finally yielded, enabling me to lift away a section large enough to admit us. I flashed my light downward until I located the metal ladder leading down into the shaft exactly where it was on the blueprint.

Three elevators rode side by side in the shaft. All three were now parked at ground level. Examination of the wiring diagrams had shown me that if any of them were moved, an alarm would be set off. Similarly, if any of the elevator doors on each floor leading to the shaft were opened, the result would be the same. To avoid setting off an alarm, we had to confine our activities to the shaft itself.

This was no handicap. The architect's plans had revealed that the back wall of the elevator shaft at street level was also the rear wall of the bank vault. It could never have happened in the US, but evidently the Bahamians were more casual about that sort of thing. It meant we wouldn't have to leave the elevator shaft until we were ready to enter the bank vault.

I hadn't explained any of this to Erikson. Sometimes a deviation from set plans is required in an emergency, and if a participant recognizes the deviation but not the emergency, nervousness results. Erikson didn't know how I proposed to do the job he had coaxed me to do for him when he had flown out to Hazel Andrews' ranch near Ely, Nevada.

Hazel is my girl friend, all redheaded six feet of her, and Karl Erikson was no stranger to us. He was a government agent linked to an unnamed Washington operation that had seemingly limitless latitude in its maneuverings. He had moved into my life obliquely at a time when I was engaged in masterminding the quiet removal of a large chunk of charming money cached in a museum in Castro's Havana.

The man who set up the deal presented Karl Erikson to me as part of a four-man team of cons and ex-cons brought together specifically to abstract the cash. By the time I found out Erikson was intent upon recovering the same cash for the Treasury Department (to whom in a roundabout way it belonged), he and Hazel and I were in the drink somewhere between Havana and Key West, choking on briny sea water and ducking cannon fire from angry Cuban MIGs.

The resultant mutual rescue operation cemented the three-sided acquaintance, and Erikson didn't hesitate to call upon me again to utilize skills I hadn't developed in a monastery. I never knew how he explained his employment of me to his unnamed bosses. Perhaps he didn't try, since he was a Viking-style pragmatist who relied on letting results speak for themselves. He was also the strongest man I had ever known.

The task of moving all our equipment down the shaft and depositing it on top of one of the elevator cabs was almost as much work as it had been to get it up to the roof. Erikson served as chief loadbearer again. I followed him down the narrow steel ladder after replacing the removed tin section of floor above my head. Standing on the ladder, I fastened it from below with a single sheet metal screw.

We were sealed inside the elevator shaft now until the job was done. Or until something went wrong, and they came looking for us.

Erikson stared at me expectantly when we were standing together on the top of the elevator that operated adjacent to the back wall of the vault. "What happens now?" he wanted to know. His voice echoed hollowly in the shaft.

"We go to work," I informed him.

Elevators always have an emergency door in their roofs. I raised the door, wriggled through the opening, and dropped down inside. Erikson handed our bulky equipment down to me before thudding down onto the carpeted floor beside me. "Shall I close the door in the top of the elevator?" he asked in a half-whisper.

"No," I said in a normal tone. "We'll need the ventilation." Erikson was going to have to get used to hearing a lot more noise before he heard less.

I located the light switch on the car's control panel and turned on the overhead light. Then I unloaded our canvas sacks and spread their contents in a semicircle on the floor of the cab. I picked up a magnetized screwdriver and removed the screws from one of the three-by-seven-foot metal panels making up the back of the car. I lifted it out of the way, thereby exposing the reinforced concrete wall of the vault just a foot away.

Next I cut the heads from the screws I'd taken from the panel and glued them back in place on the face of the panel with contact cement. Erikson watched me with a puzzled look.

I reached up and removed the light bulb in the roof of the car. Erikson held my penlight so I could see what I was doing while I installed a two-socket fixture. I put the bulb in one socket and a female plug in the other. Now that I had both light and a source of power, I plugged in my masonry drill and attacked the wall of the vault.

The concrete was fourteen inches thick, but the drill chewed through it like a run in a fat girl's pantyhose. I soon had the wall honeycombed with holes. Erikson watched intently. "It can't be this easy," he said.

"It's not," I told him. "There's quarter-inch steel plate behind that concrete."

From the floor of the cab I selected three lengths of steel pipe, which I screwed together to make a handle. To this I attached a solid twelve-pound weight that completed the birth of a heavy striking implement. I handed the sledge to Erikson. "Go ahead, muscles," I invited him. "Bust up that concrete."

"What about noise?"

"The watchman will hear it, but if it's done quickly enough, he won't be able to get a fix on it. Then he'll rationalize that it came from outside."

Erikson went at it with long-armed, gorillalike swings of the sledge and soon had the air laden with powdery dust. Even before I removed the panel, there was a one-foot space between the vault wall and the back of the elevator cab. Most of the concrete chunks and chips from Erikson's sledging operation fell into this gap and ended up at the bottom of the shaft, but some debris was sprayed around the floor of the cab.

Erikson worked so rapidly and to such good effect that he soon exposed the latticework of reinforcing rods, which was all that separated us from the steel vault liner. I stopped him while I disconnected the masonry drill we wouldn't need again. I plugged in a miniature hand-held vacuum cleaner and began to clean up some of the mess we'd made in the cab.

Anything too large to be sucked into the cleaner we kicked over the edge into the bottom of the shaft. I turned the cleaner onto our clothing to remove the clinging dust, paying special attention to the welt of our shoes. I had made sure that our trousers were cuffless.

I laid the vacuum aside and picked up my acetylene outfit. Like all my tools except the masonry drill, it was both lightweight and compact. The hose was only six feet long, the gauges were miniature, the acetylene was carried in a small propane tank, and the oxygen was contained in a pair of skin-diving tanks. The outfit was big enough to do the required job but without much to spare.

I took up a knitted ski mask and slipped it over my head. I checked pressure gauges and cutting torch size before lighting the torch. It had a hot, violet flame that in seconds turned the reinforcement rods to water. When I heated them up and squeezed the oxygen handle, the metal grew red, then yellow, then ruptured, and ran before the invisible jet of oxygen.

The barrier of rods separating us from the vault liner was soon just short lengths of twisted scrap metal at the bottom of the elevator shaft. I inspected the final obstacle, the steel liner. From outside it looked like any other piece of steel plate, but I knew from my study of the architect's drawings there was no way I could cut through it without setting off an alarm.

"When I burn this and climb down inside there," I told Erikson, "clean up everything in the cab again after you pass the equipment inside to me. The cab has to look as though it hasn't been used for anything. Get set to go. When we move now, we move fast."

Erikson stacked the equipment to one side of the removed cab panel. I connected the second oxygen tank, readjusted the torch, took a deep breath, and sliced through the steel vault liner plate in one long cut, following the edges of the sledged-away concrete.

When the outline was completed, I kicked hard at the center portion of the vault liner. The torched section fell inside the vault with a sound like a Chinese gong. "Quick now!" I said to Erikson. Bells were ringing all over town. I didn't know how many minutes we had before watchmen, security guards, and police would be crawling all over the building.

Erikson had the vacuum going again feverishly while I grabbed up a can of air freshener. I closed the emergency exit in the cab's roof and sprayed the inside of the car with the aerosol bomb before dropping the can into the pit and jumping down through the hole we'd made into the vault's interior. The aerosol spray would remove the last traces of torch heat and cement dust from the elevator.

Erikson began handing the equipment in to me over the hot edge of the gaping hole in the vault liner. When I had it all, he scrambled down into the vault. I reached back up and fitted the previously unscrewed back wall panel from the cab into place again, working from inside the vault and outside the elevator. I fastened the panel into place firmly using half a dozen powerful Alnico magnets. From inside the cab there was nothing to show the panel had ever been removed, since I'd glued the cut-off screw heads back in place, and the panel was almost as securely attached from the rear by the magnets as it would have been by the original screws.

"Now what?" Erikson asked tensely. We could hear the sound of running feet outside the vault entrance. I could picture the watchman, perplexed at the sudden explosion of sound, checking to make sure it was unopened. And being relieved to find the status quo.

"We wait," I told Erikson.

"Like rabbits in a snare?" he demanded. He sounded as though he didn't care much for the idea.

"Like pigs in clover," I tried to soothe him. "Until they search the building and satisfy themselves there's nothing wrong. There never was an alarm system in the world that didn't kick itself off accidentally at some time or other, and eventually the security guards and the police will conclude that's what happened now."

Erikson shook his head dubiously. More voices could be heard outside the vault. They seemed to be shouting at each other. Some were close to the vault door, and some sounded as though they were reaching us through the hole in the wall of the elevator shaft. This was confirmed when the elevator started upward suddenly with a grinding noise.

When it was a floor above us, I leaned out through the hole in the vault's steel liner and aimed my light downward into the shaft. The debris at the bottom didn't appear at all unusual. There's often a lot of construction rubble at the base of such shafts, and this one had obviously had quite a bit before we added our contribution to it. Bricks, boards, mortar, and miscellaneous waste surrounded the large shock absorber in the pit.

Excited voices aboard the elevator harangued each

other in rich British accents. "Search all floors immejitly!" an authoritative, clipped voice commanded brusquely. The elevator rose still higher, and we could hear voices rising and falling as the order was carried out.

I peeled off the surgeon's rubber gloves I was wearing. My hands had been perspiring inside the thin latex, and the flesh of my fingertips felt like uncooked prunes, they were so puckered from the moisture.

Erikson was still listening intently as the voices from the shaft called back and forth to each other. "How long is this damned commotion going to last?" he asked irritably. He held an unlighted cigarette in his rubber-gloved right hand.

"Not much longer," I said confidently. "They'll get tired of playing Boy Scout. We'll have plenty of time before the bank opens for business." I beamed my light around the corners of the vault until I located a steel-strapped money chest. I sat down on it and rested my back gratefully against a wall patterned with safe deposit box drawers. "Go ahead and light up."

"Won't someone smell it?" he asked doubtfully. "A draft could draw the smoke through the hole you burned in the vault liner and carry it up the elevator shaft."

"Half of them will be smoking anyhow, Karl."

He hesitated another moment, then lit up. He spoke again after the first expelled lungful of smoke wreathed his square-chinned, bulldog features and rough-looking blond hair. "I've got to hand it to you, Earl. The one place they'll never think to look for us is inside the vault itself." He took another deep drag on his cigarette before extinguishing it and dropping the butt into his shirt pocket. "How long will it take you to get into the safe deposit boxes?"

"No time at all. Nothing like what it would take to get inside this money chest I'm sitting on."

"We're not here for that!" he said sharply.

"You never did tell me why we're here," I pointed out.

He didn't answer me.

It hadn't taken Karl Erikson long to get to the point when he showed up at Hazel's ranch in the copper-mining district of eastern Nevada a month ago. Out of Hazel's hearing he informed me that his as-always-unspecified bosses in Washington had handed him the assignment of procuring an unnamed something from a couple of safe deposit boxes in a bank vault in Nassau.

"I told them I couldn't even consider making the attempt unless I could pick the man to go with me," Karl said earnestly when we were alone in front of the barn where I was gassing up the rented car in which he'd driven from Reno. There's a United flight daily from San Francisco into the Ely airport which goes on to Salt Lake City and vice versa, but if you miss them, you wait twenty-four hours. Karl Erikson didn't have that kind of patience. "But after what happened to the Turk on our last job, the head man didn't want to okay it when I named you," he continued. "He finally gave in when I insisted no one else could swing the job."

"Did you ever consider I might like the option of saying 'No' sometimes before you volunteer me for one of your projects?" I had asked a bit warmly.

"Ahhhhh, come on, Earl. There just isn't anyone on our books who can match your talent for this job."

"Flattery will get you nowhere," I told him firmly.

But of course it had.

Plus the fact I owed Karl Erikson a couple of favors difficult to repay in ordinary coin.

He knew what I'd been. Not in detail, but he knew. He was a complete opportunist when it came to carrying out his orders, though, and he had no qualms about using me. Not that our prior relationship had been a one-way street. Karl Erikson drew a lot of water in the underground levels of government where he operated—a situation which in the light of my past afforded a substantial umbrella when he was on my side.

He was a hard man to say no to and make it stick. He was that truly hard-to-find individual, a dedicated man in the service of his country, and so closemouthed that it should really have been no surprise to me that I sat beside him inside a Nassau bank vault and still had no idea why we were there.

I had my own ideas, of course. If I'd still been in business for myself, Nassau was just the type of banking situation I might have taken a hard look at. Along with Switzerland, Spain, and Hong Kong it had become both a tax haven and a repository for undeclared income. There should be some juicy stacks of bills in the safe deposit boxes against which my back was resting.

The sound of voices was diminishing outside the vault. Erikson paced, not nervously but impatiently. His head was cocked to one side as he listened. "I'm curious," he said finally, coming to a halt in front of me. "What alternative plan did you have if anything had gone wrong and we couldn't get out of the vault before the building opened in the morning and the elevators were in use, pinning us here?"

"Simple," I said. "I'd have jammed the vault's timing mechanism from inside here. I'd have jammed it so badly it would have taken technicians a couple of days to open the twenty-ton door. If the bank personnel couldn't open the door, they couldn't know we were here, and we'd have gone out over the roof again after the building closed tonight. You said the plane would be showing up once every twenty-four hours for three days, so we'd just have been set back a day. That's the only thing that could have gone wrong."

"Speaking of things going wrong," Erikson said. "If only one of us makes it in the plane to Andrews Field in Washington, we're to meet a man named Baker and turn the material over to him. He'll be there each of the next three days from 8:00 to 8:10 A.M."

I waved it aside. "The only thing that bothers me is that we've got to hide out for a day now before the plane shows up and this is a damned small island."

"Eighty square miles," Erikson said soberly.

"Oh well, we've made up before for shortcomings of the Washington brain bank," I philosophized. "We'll manage this time, too."

"Nothing like working with a professional," Erikson said drily. There were no sounds now from outside the vault. "Are we ready?"

"Relax. Let's give the police time to get back in the sack after giving the security people hell for rousting them out."

We both fell silent. For half an hour the only sound inside the vault was our breathing. Finally I stood up, drawing on my rubber gloves again. "Okay," I said. "What are we after?"

Erikson took my thin-beamed light and shined it on the rows of safe deposit boxes. The beam traveled in a short arc, returned, then repeated its passage. "These three," Erikson said. "Numbers C-114, C-115, and C-116."

I moved in more closely and examined the twin locks on the boxes. They were quite ordinary. Who puts expensive locks on safe deposit boxes inside a vault? Not the banks in Nassau, anyway.

"No problem," I assured Erikson. I went to our equipment and selected a U-shaped steel punch. I picked up a ball-peen hammer also and then approached the boxes again.

Speed was important now because the next noise we made was going to convince an already nervous watchman that things weren't kosher. I hoped he was stationed close to the vault door where the thicknesses of steel and solid concrete would help to muffle noise. If the police had left a second man in the lobby near the elevator doors, there was no way he could miss hearing us. There was nothing we could do about it except move fast.

I positioned the punch over the twin lock of box C-114, took a short grip on the hammer, and swung it hard. The contact sounded like a bomb going off in the confined space of the vault. The box drawer sagged open drunkenly, its lock mechanism pulverized.

Erikson shook his head. "I thought Jock McLaren was good with locks, but he could go to your school." He lifted the cover from the box and began to scoop its contents into a small canvas sack. The contents seemed to be mostly loose papers and not too many of them.

Jock McLaren was one of Erikson's men who had been with us at the finale when a fat Turk took an unhealthy interest in an AEC shipment from Hanford, Washington, that was being trucked across the country. "Seen Jock lately?" I asked as I placed the punch over the lock of C-115. BOOOOONNNNNGGGG! The box sprang open.

"I had dinner with him and his wife a few weeks ago at their home in Arlington, Virginia," Erikson said as he rifled the second box.

C-116 required two blows from the hammer instead of one. Otherwise the results were the same. It was like poking three winners in a row from a huge punchboard. "That's it?" I asked Erikson as he flattened papers inside the canvas sack to make it more manageable.

"That's it." He knotted a cord around the neck of the sack, which bulged hardly at all.

There had been no sound from outside the vault. The whole affair hardly seemed worth the trouble. I looked with regret at the rows and rows of additional boxes and the money chests scattered around the floor of the vault. "You sure we're not mad at this bank? It could be a hell of a nice touch."

"We're ready to leave," Erikson said emphatically.

"You're the doctor," I surrendered. "Don't bother about the tools. We won't be taking most of them. Don't forget to write off the expense on your next income tax return."

Erikson snorted as I selected a screwdriver and an eigh-teen-inch crowbar from the tools on the floor and returned to the entrance hole we'd made in the back of the vault. The magnets I'd used to hold the elevator's loosened back wall panel in place were too strong for me to pull away with my hands, but I pried them free with the crowbar. I shoved the panel out of the way.

I stepped up into the cab and Erikson followed right behind me. "Quietly now," I cautioned. "Anyone listening can hear us a lot more plainly in this thing than through the vault thicknesses."

I reached above my head to push open the emergency door in the elevator roof, then froze. Just above my up-stretched hands the elevator light still glowed, and it illumi-nated brilliantly the two-way fixture I'd installed to pro-vide both light and a power source.

Erikson saw the direction of my glance, and his brow corrugated when he spotted the fixture. "Goddamnit," he said softly, "I forgot to take it out. Of all the stupid—"

"I should have reminded you," I cut in.

"I shouldn't have needed to be reminded!" he growled. "You told me the cab had to look as though no one had been aboard it. I could have blown the whole bit by for-getting to remove that fixture."

A sharp-eyed cop could certainly have earned himself a promotion. I wondered uneasily if a sharp-eyed cop *was* going to earn himself a promotion. If the tell-tale fixture had been noticed and the roof of the bank building and the street outside were staked out by silent, waiting Bahamian police . . .

I reached under my jacket and loosened my .38 in its shoulder holster. "There's going to be one hell of a scramble if the police are waiting for us on the roof, Karl. I think we'd better—"

A smashing blow on the muscle of my right arm numbed the arm and slammed me up against the side of the elevator cab. Karl Erikson's big hand snaked inside my jacket and emerged with my .38. "No shooting!" he said harshly.

"No shooting?" I echoed incredulously as the numbness vanished and pain flooded my entire right side. "Goddamn you, Karl, I'm not going to rot in a stinking—"

"I said no shooting," he repeated but in a quieter tone. "This is a friendly government. Maybe they didn't notice anything. Get up the ladder."

We certainly had to do that anyway. I shoved open the emergency door in the cab's roof and pulled myself up through the opening with Erikson assisting me from below. I needed assistance; the big bastard had just about decommissioned me with one punch. I helped him up when I was standing on the elevator roof. The pain in my right arm seemed to be increasing steadily. Erikson had a fist with the impact of a jackhammer.

I transferred the screwdriver to a jacket pocket and the crowbar to a hanging loop on my vest before I started up the steel ladder. I used my left hand to pull myself upward. At the top of the shaft I unscrewed the single screw I'd left to hold the loosened piece of tin flooring, then pushed the square of metal aside.

I reached still further upward with only the upper part of my body through the opening and feet still on the ladder rungs. I could hear the sounds of Erikson's scuffling ascent below me as I leaned forward and put a hand on the door and gently cracked open the entrance to the small structure housing the elevator mechanism.

It was still dark outside but not the total blackness of several hours before. A tinge of gray in the eastern sky hinted at the approaching dawn. Everything seemed quiet on the rooftop. I took a relieved breath and raised a foot to the next ladder rung.

And then through the crack I saw at the farthest perimeter of the roof a dark face appear suddenly in the quick glow of a lighted cigarette held in a cupped hand.

TWO

I DROPPED down inside the shaft, then bent nearly double on the ladder to get closer to Erikson. "They're on the roof!" I whispered. "Give me the gun!" His response was to remove my .38 from a pocket and drop it down the elevator shaft. I heard the dull thud of its landing on the roof of the elevator. "Goddamnit, Karl—!"

"Shut up!" His response was more rasp than whisper. "We've got to get clear with this sack. Here. You take it." He thrust it at me. "I'll meet you at the airstrip rendezvous this time tomorrow morning if we become separated. If only one of us makes it, remember the name *Baker* at Andrews at eight A.M. Now change places with me. I'm going out first."

"What the hell difference does it make who goes out first? Climb back down and get my gun, and I'll—"

"Shut up and do as I say!"

We changed places on the ladder in a grisly ballet of sweaty, grasping hands and bumping bodies. Perspiration was crawling down my back by the time Erikson scrambled past me on the narrow ladder. I made a loop in the cord around the neck of the sack and hung it around my neck after ripping off my tool-carrying vest and dropping it into the elevator pit. I held onto the ladder with one hand while I buttoned my jacket over the sack with the other. Its bulk didn't seem too conspicuous, and it left both my hands free.

Erikson pulled himself upward until he could straddle the opening in the floor. Then he burst through the door and went out across the roof in a bulllike rush. I was still trying to pull myself up through the hole when I heard excited shouts and the sounds of heavy bodies colliding violently.

Bobbing flashlight beams played upon a totally disorganized scene when I reached the doorway. Erikson's initial charge had taken him nearly to the edge of the roof, opposite the way we had gained it. He was enveloped in a cloud of men, but his muscular body kept shedding them like a dog flinging off water drops.

All attention was fixed upon the melee. Men in uniform danced around its edges, trying to get into the action. I knew that I was supposed to take advantage of Erikson's delaying action. I eased out the door and started across the roof toward the open space between the buildings.

A hand clutched my arm tightly as I approached the roof's edge. I hadn't even seen the man until I felt the hand, but I caught a glimpse of a uniform sleeve with stripes on it. "Follow me, Sergeant!" I got out in as much of a tone of command as I could muster. "There's another one on the next roof!"

The hand fell away. I didn't look around. I took two long strides followed by two loping ones, then leaped across the gap. My challenger landed almost on my heels, but I was ready for him. I hand bladed the back of his neck solidly as he came down in a half-crouched position. He grunted heavily as he plowed up the roof's tarred surface with his face, rolled over, and then collapsed motionless.

There was no one on the second roof. I trotted down the rear fire escape while the sounds of battle from the roof of the bank building echoed clearly in the predawn stillness. My conservatively cut business suit had passed me at first glance, but I knew I couldn't stand a close inspection. I might not look like a bank robber, but I surely resembled a man who had had a long, hard night.

Just before I dropped down from the final section of fire escape into the littered alley, the sounds from the roof of the bank ceased. I knew that Karl Erikson wouldn't be meeting me at the airstrip rendezvous the following morning.

And I knew I wasn't in much better shape myself.

I had to find someplace to hide for twenty-four hours until Erikson's pilot made the rendezvous. I had to hide while every cop in and out of uniform shook down the tiny island looking for me.

I moved along the alley for three-quarters of a block, remaining in the deeper shadow of the building walls. I turned into a narrow side passage and hurried to Shirley Street. I stopped just short of the sidewalk and looked up the street. In front of the bank police cars and jeeps were parked at odd angles with red and orange spinner lights flickering like a kaleidoscope gone mad.

I left the security of the alley entrance and walked in the opposite direction as leisurely as my hard-pumping adrenalin gland and perspiration-itching scars would permit. I was trying to hold down the surge of bitter anger at the thought of a single mistake that had blown a perfect job. Anger wouldn't solve anything. Because of the mistake Karl Erikson was in custody, and I was going to be hard put not to join him.

I couldn't stand any sort of inquiry. Passports and visas aren't required in the Bahamas, but proof of identity in the form of a birth certificate or something similar is a necessity. Neither Erikson nor I had anything of the sort, of course. We had stripped ourselves of all possible means of identification. We had even removed clothing labels.

I was automatically in trouble the first time I couldn't produce proof of identity for anyone requesting it. I had to get off the street at the earliest possible moment, and I had nowhere to go. I couldn't check into a hotel without identification, and dressed as I was, I could hardly go to the beach. The stores wouldn't open for another three or four hours, and the gambling casino on Paradise Island didn't open until midafternoon.

I zigzagged away from the trouble spot, turning onto Victoria Avenue from Shirley Street. I passed Dowdeswell Street before reaching Bay, where I turned east. Another two blocks brought me to Rawson Square, one of the centers of business activity.

I stood indecisively in the square near a carriage stand under a mango tree. An increasing number of early-morning risers proceeding along the sidewalks kept me from feeling quite so noticeable. Smiling black men on bicycles, wearing white uniforms with open-throated white shirts, hailed each other in soft Bahamian accents. They were apparently hotel employees on their way to work. "Hey, mon!" one called cheerfully across the street to a friend. "See you at the party tonight, righto?"

The clipped British-sounding voice reminded me of something. When I had recently been on a chartered flight to Las Vegas for professional gamblers, one of the more prominent crap shooters on the plane had been a stocky, smiling black man in a lime green suit, lime green suede shoes, lime green derby hat, and a pink ruffled shirt. And the black man had spoken in just such a clipped British-sounding inflection.

Duke Conboy, my sponsor on the flight, explained that the man's accent was due to the fact that he was from Nassau in the Bahamas. And here was I in Nassau in the Bahamas.

But what was the man's name?

I couldn't remember.

I stepped into a doorway while I tried to think. The first name had been a nickname, I was sure of that. But what? I recalled his rugged-looking, black features perfectly. When our plane was hijacked by three hophead

Palestinian Arabs, I had been able to get out on a wing following a near-crash landing and shoot down two of them. It hadn't prevented a third from departing with our cash in a private plane stationed at the hijack spot for that purpose.

The Arabs had killed the plane crew after the hijack, including the stewardess. One of the men I shot was dead when the enraged gamblers poured out of the grounded plane. A slashing razor in the hands of the black man had seen to it that the second Arab didn't survive long.

But what was the black man's name?

I stood there in the shelter of the shop doorway while the sunlight crept down the building fronts across the street, trying to recall the details of Duke Conboy's introduction of me to the black man at Kennedy Airport just before we boarded the ill-fated 727 gambling flight. And then the image of Duke's middle-aged choirboy features with a cigar stub set firmly in the center of his cherubic countenance brought the incident swimming up from my subconscious.

Kane.

That was the name.

Candy Kane, gambler deluxe from Nassau.

And if I could locate him, I might still have a chance of pulling off this project.

I inspected myself in the shop window which served as a mirror. The suit was badly wrinkled after the night's activities. The hair was no problem since it was a wig. An expensive wig. My beard has never been a problem since I spent a year undergoing plastic surgery after an automobile gas tank blew up in my face while I was standing off a bunch of sheriff's deputies. My beard doesn't grow now. On the whole I didn't think I looked too much worse than any male tourist who might have intentionally strayed from travel-agent-recommended channels to find a little excitement on his own.

I moved out of the doorway and down Bay Street. One

of the hotels would do for a starting point in the search for
Candy Kane—any of the larger ones. I angled back toward the beach and turned in between the impressive
white pillars of the Anchorage.

The lobby was enveloped in an early-morning hush. I
went to a bank of public phones and turned to the *K*s in
the directory. There were seven *Kanes,* but no *Candy.* No
first names of the *Kanes* that began with a *C,* even.
But then would a man in Candy's line of business be listed
in the phone book?

I closed the phone directory and started across the
lobby. "Sorry, sair," a white-jacketed black bellboy called
out to me as my heels click-clicked on the tiles. "The
coffee shop won't be open for anothair hour."

I headed toward him, fingering a bill loose from the
folded-over roll in my pocket. I withdrew my hand and
gave the boy a flash of the green in it before I spoke. "I'm
trying to locate a friend," I said. "His name is Candy
Kane." The boy said nothing. "He's been known to do a
little gambling."

That broke the ice. "He has indeed, sair, if we are
speakin' of the same mon." The bellboy sounded amused.
"But the Candy Kane I know is—" He hesitated.

"Black," I supplied. "Rugged. Five ten. Two hundred
pounds." The boy nodded at each item. I held out the
bill to him. "What's Candy's address?"

He made no move to accept the bill. "I can tell you
where to reach Candy, sair. Then if he wishes to give you
his address, that's his business."

"Fair enough. Where do I reach him?"

The bellboy lifted the back of his white jacket and
removed a wallet from his hip pocket. From it he extracted a white card which he handed to me. The card was
a cheaply printed rectangle with the edges of its black
lettering smudged. Large letters in the center said CANDY
KANE. Smaller letters in the upper left corner said ROY. In

the lower left corner it said GAMES OF CHANCE, and in the lower right corner was a phone number.

"I'm Roy," the bellboy offered.

"Fine, Roy," I said and completed the transfer of the bill to his hand. I didn't know if I'd been lucky enough to stumble onto one of Candy's steerers, or whether he had his cards in the wallets of all black hotel employees on the island. I didn't care.

I went back to the public phones and called the number on the card. There were five or six rings before anyone answered. "Yes?" a feminine voice inquired in a drawn-out note of inquiry.

"I'd like to speak to Candy Kane."

"Tell him we're closed, baby," a rich baritone voice that I recognized said in the background.

"Tell Candy that Earl Drake wants to speak to him," I urged.

There was a short silence, and then the baritone reverberated in my ear. "Do I know an Earl Drake?"

"You do."

"Where'd you get this number?"

"From Roy."

"Where'd I know an Earl Drake?"

"You remember him from a plane flight to Vegas. He was with Duke Conboy."

The baritone soared. "Oh, mon, do I remember! Do I ever remember! I ain't been well financially since. You heah for long? You want to come over tonight for some action?"

"I want to come over right now."

There was another silence. "Your clock's all turned around, Earl. The action broke up heah two hours ago. We're jus' partyin'."

I had already detected a thickened syllable or two in Candy's speech. "I don't want to party, but I do want to talk to you. Right now. Alone."

"Well—" The baritone sounded undecided. "Where you at?"

"The Anchorage."

"Oh, yeah. You did say Roy. Well, if you don't mind walkin', chappie, it's a dozen blocks. I don't care to have no vee-hickles pullin' up in front in daylight, okay? It's 325 Eurydice Street. Roy will tell you how to get here. Second floor up. Ground floor's a massage parlor."

"I'll be right there," I said and hung up the phone.

Roy was at my elbow when I turned away from the booth. "It's off Elizabeth Avenue near the Queen's Stairway," he explained and added detailed directions. I laid another bill on him and left the lobby of the Anchorage.

The sun was already high enough to be inching the temperature upward toward its daily average of seventy-eight degrees. I held my pace down to avoid calling undue attention to myself among the easy-striding Bahamians. If I could just get under cover at Candy's until Erikson's scheduled plane was due to arrive at the private airstrip, I felt I had it made.

Eurydice Street was a narrow lane lined with small shops, most of them with whitewashed fronts. I found the place without difficulty. A sign on the small ground floor window said CHEN YI'S MASSAGE PARLOR in red-and-gold lettering. A line below it said BY APPOINTMENT ONLY. The door was locked, but to the right of it was another door in the same building. It opened when I tried it, and I looked up a flight of narrow stairs.

The stairwell was considerably cooler than the street outside. At the top of the flight I was confronted by another locked door. It felt solid when I knocked upon it. There was a momentary delay while an inside panel slipped open and someone examined me through one-way glass as I stood on the shadowed landing. Then I heard the sound of bolts snicking from their sockets before the door opened wide.

Candy Kane grabbed my right hand in his powerful one

and practically dragged me inside. There was little light in the tiny entranceway, and it took me a second to realize that Candy's muscular body was attired solely in a casually draped towel. Sweat glistened upon his ebony skin. "Hey, mon!" he exclaimed exuberantly with the island's all-purpose greeting. He gave every indication of enthusiasm despite my having forced myself upon him. "You're lookin' fit!"

"Can we talk here, Candy?"

"Jus' soon's I take care of this," he said promptly. He slammed the bolts back into position after closing the door. I could see that the door itself was three or four panels thick and had metal plate screwed to the inside. "Like to be able to control who walks in an' out've here of an evenin'," Candy continued with a wink.

His eyes were red rimmed, and he wasn't articulating too well, but he didn't sound drunk. From somewhere in the background my nostrils picked up a trace of the sweetness of marijuana. Candy leaned back until his broad shoulders were resting upon the closed door. He wasn't tall, but he was remarkably thick through the body without being at all fat. "So?" he said expectantly.

"I need a place to stay. Unofficially."

There was no change in his expression, but the red-rimmed eyes examined me more carefully. "How long?"

I had been about to say twenty-four hours. The sight of Candy's security arrangements, though, had triggered a new line of thought. "Not more than three or four days."

"What you runnin' from?"

"The law."

"Mainland?"

"Local."

He cocked an eyebrow. "How'd you git crossways locally? Well, never mind. How you gonna git off the island?"

"It's all arranged."

He considered the implications of that for a moment,

sucking air through a gap in his strong-looking white teeth. "It don't seem to be a real problem," he said at last.

"You hold your games here?"

He nodded. "But I've an extra room I can slip you into, an' nobody'll know you're around. Nobody that'd bother you."

"You don't sound as British as some I've heard around here," I suggested. "Roy, for instance."

Candy grinned again. "I worked six years in Miami. Stick man for a casino crap game."

"Why don't the police bother you here?"

He rubbed a thumb and forefinger together. *"Baksheesh.* It gets me by so long as I don't go after the high rollers headin' for the casino." He moved away from the door. "C'mon inside an' meet the girls."

"Girls?"

But he was already beyond the entranceway and striding into the room beyond.

I followed.

It was like another world.

The room was large, and it gave the immediate impression of being one into which sunlight never penetrated. Heavy draperies shielded all the windows. Flickering candles in ornate holders supplied the only light. Joss sticks burned beside the candles, and the odor of incense eddied through the room, combined with the aroma of pot.

Low couches displaying pastel fabrics were the room's predominant items of furniture. There were no chairs. Lacquered screens were set carelessly at odd angles. The rug was deep pile, and in the center of the surprising room, incongruously enough, was a full-sized gymnasium mat of the type used by wrestlers.

"This chappie is a friend of mine, girls," Candy announced. "His name is Earl. Say hello, Chen Yi."

A girl rose from a petal-pink couch. And rose and rose and rose. She was barefooted but still towered six inches above Candy and me. She was Chinese with long, straight, black hair framing a beautiful face. There is nothing in the world as black as a Chinese girl's hair.

There was a lot more of the girl bare than her feet, because her costume consisted solely of a choke-collared, Russian-style blouse that ended at her waist. I looked at her, looked away, then looked back again. Her body was spectacular. "Hello, Earl," she said softly.

"Hi," I returned weakly.

"An' this bit of fluff is Consuelo," Candy went on. He pointed to another couch where a brown-haired girl was reclining. She was smoking a water pipe, and her pupils were dilated. Consuelo was almost as Spanish looking as her name except that her eyes were slanted like a Polynesian's, and her skin tone was almond rather than *café au lait*. It wasn't hard to make the analysis since her attire consisted of one hundred percent less material than that of Chen Yi, the Chinese girl. Consuelo waved languidly from her couch. I waved back.

"An' Hermione," Candy said, pulling aside a lacquered screen. A third girl stared up at me from a supine position on a third couch, her doe eyes glazed with a marijuana euphoria. She was a flaxen blonde, a butterball of a girl with the high facial coloring and flawless pale skin associated with English mists and moors. She was wearing a terrycloth towel like Candy's and a dreamy smile. Her taut nipples were strawberry splashes against the creamy expanse of her tip-tilted breasts.

"How about a spot of cheer?" Candy asked me.

I started to refuse, then thought better of it. A cold-sober approach to life seemed too wildly at variance with the relaxed attitudes in this extraordinary room. "Brandy, if you have it. And thanks."

"Chen Yi," Candy said.

The tall girl went to a cabinet near one wall and took down a bottle of brandy. I estimated her height at four inches above six feet. I could see that the brandy was Metaxa. Chen Yi poured liberally into a bell-shaped snifter. I couldn't remove my gaze from the broad acreage of her fully disclosed ivory buttocks.

"A joint?" Candy inquired.

"Not right now," I evaded the issue. So far I've managed to get my kicks in life without employing Mary Jane.

"We were jus' workin' out," Candy continued with a nod at the gymnasium mat. "Burns out the poisons. Slide onto a couch. We'll talk more later. C'mon, Chen Yi."

Hermione, the blonde, patted the couch beside herself invitingly. I sat down, lowering myself cautiously until I found myself barely a foot above the luxuriant carpeting, careful not to spill the fine Greek brandy. At the first sip its warmth traveled from my throat to my stomach so rapidly it reminded me it was quite a few hours since I'd eaten.

Candy stepped onto the gym mat wearing only his loosely knotted towel. Chen Yi advanced to meet him, still clad in her abbreviated high-necked blouse. Candy was a bear of a man, built close to the ground. He faced the girl with his legs apart in a semicrouched position with his weight on the balls of his feet. His hands rested lightly on his thighs. I had taken judo instruction once, and I recognized the stance as judo's main defensive posture, the *jigo-hontai*.

The Chinese girl confronted Candy drawn up to her full height, her arms slightly away from her body. This was the *shizen-hontai,* judo's so called natural posture. She charged Candy suddenly, attempting to unbalance him, but he took her down with a classic knee wheel that rolled her completely over.

While on the mat she did something with her feet, too quick for me to follow anything except smoothly rippling muscles in thighs and buttocks. Candy sprawled heavily beside her, and they both sprang to their feet and faced off again in reverse postures.

A touch on my thigh brought my head around as I took

another swallow of brandy. Hermione's towel had disappeared completely, and she was snuggling closer to me. I slipped an arm around her, and the silky skin of her waist titillated my fingertips. The bushy triangle of her body hair was as blond as her head. "Where are you from?" she asked drowsily.

"Washington," I said. It was the first thing that came into my head, and it was true enough since Erikson and I had taken off from Andrews Field.

A thudding sound drew my attention to the mat again. I drank brandy and watched the strange contest. Candy and Chen Yi took turns on offense and defense. He may have been stronger, but not by much, and she was quicker. She appeared to have enormous strength in her hands and upper body. She was even better at the *hiza-guruma,* the knee wheel, than Candy was. Both worked hard at attempting to get the opponent off-balance before trying to apply their own holds. The flying black and yellow bodies crashed to the mat in almost equal ratios.

I knew the brandy was getting to me when the ebony-and-gold ballet on the mat started to blur at the edges. And the conditions of the contest seemed to have changed. I leaned forward to see better. Instead of judo's freewheeling throws Candy and Chen Yi were working in close to each other. Arm movements were short and choppy, and both seemed to be holding back. I had never seen anything like it before.

I felt a tugging at my waist. I had slumped back without realizing it, and Hermione had my shoes off and was working on my pants. I felt marvelously relaxed, but then a slight crackling sound beneath my jacket reminded me I still had Erikson's sack. I set my snifter down on the floor while I captured Hermione's roving hands. She pouted attractively and after a moment left the couch.

Chen Yi appeared beside me and refilled my brandy glass. She was slick with perspiration, and her heavy breathing agitated the full breasts—much fuller than Hermione's even—beneath her blouse. When I started to speak to her, I found I had to shape the words carefully. My lips felt slack. "What was that you two were doing at the end, Chen Yi?"

"That is *gung fu,*" she answered. "It is not play."

I had never heard of *gung fu,* but I made a mental note to learn more. Chen Yi departed. Somewhere in the background I could hear a shower running. I picked up the brandy snifter and sampled its contents again, savoring the quick spreading warmth.

Muffled giggles drew my attention to the wrestling mat again. Consuelo and Hermione, both nude, were wrestling in one corner of it. There was no science to it, merely kittenish exuberance as the soft bodies writhed and strained together. The emphasis was purely sexual. Or impurely.

Candy Kane had materialized again. He sat cross-legged at the edge of the mat, a brooding black figure with a haze of marijuana smoke wreathed around his head. I could see white scar ridges on his powerful looking forearms that could have been nothing except the residue of knife fights. Chen Yi was nowhere in sight.

For the first time since I'd been in the room no one was paying any attention to me. I unbuttoned my jacket and lifted off the cord to the canvas sack from around my neck. I quickly stuffed the sack under a couch cushion. It was so far from being bulky that I wondered again if Erikson had really obtained his goal.

I took another swallow of brandy before I sank back upon the couch, my eyes along with Candy's upon the naked wrestlers.

Erikson . . .

I was going to have to do something about Karl Erikson.

One of the girls on the mat squealed shrilly, reclaiming my attention.

Then the nude wrestlers gradually went out of focus, and I didn't see anything.

I came to with a start.

Hermione had returned to my couch.

Her sleek nudity was plastered full length atop my own. I couldn't imagine where my clothes had gone. My nostrils were filled with the commingled odor of hyacinth, sandalwood, perspiration, and woman.

Hermione removed the empty brandy glass from my lax hand, then murmured something unintelligible as her fingertips traced the outline of the numerous scars on my chest from the skin transplants which had contributed to the remaking of my face. I reached down and secured a double handful of resilient gluteal amplitudes while Hermione continued to recline upon me. I kneaded her soft flesh until she turned her head with an impatient whimper and sank her sharp little teeth into my neck.

I cuffed her, and she rolled off onto the floor, dragging me with her. Our positions were reversed, which she seemed to consider an improvement. I wasn't so sure. The long night's effort and the brandy had induced a lassitude which made me doubt my response.

But Hermione had no doubts. Despite my weight upon her she performed prodigies of acrobatic movement with her pelvis as the fulcrum. She agitated me until a fleshy linchpin connected us, and her wide hips rose clear of the floor in her eagerness to meet and return each thrust.

It seemed to go on for a long time. I had the feeling at times that I was riding out a storm. The girl was a natural force. In my alcoholic haze the eventual climax felt like jumping from the haymow in a tall, tall barn.

I went plunging down and down and down and down.

And out.

I woke with a jerk and sat up abruptly.

I was back on the couch in the exotically furnished room.

Stubby candles still furnished the room's only light, and the lingering odor of incense and marijuana still remained in the air. But there was no gymnasium mat in the center of the floor and no naked female bodies entwined upon it.

And no Hermione.

I wondered if I had dreamed it all.

My mouth tasted foul enough from the brandy residue to make me feel that an alcoholic dream was far from an impossibility. But Candy Kane had been no dream. I was sure of that.

The apartment's airlessness, the brandy, and the uneasy sleep had combined to leave me well stewed in my own juices. I levered myself upright from the low couch and went in search of the bathroom from which I had heard the sound of running water.

En route I padded barefoot to the nearest window and pushed aside the elaborate draperies. Bright sunlight blinded me momentarily while I fumbled for the latch on the steel frame casement windows. I shoved them open and breathed deeply of the warm, flower scented air.

I squinted over the roofs of the single-story shops across the street and down the slope toward the waterfront. Just beyond Bay Street and Rawson Square I could see a huge white cruise ship moored against the Prince George Wharf, its gleaming superstructure in sharp contrast to the red tile roof of the customs building next to it.

The sound of wheels drew my attention to the narrow lane below. A policeman in a white tunic, his brown face made darker by the shade afforded by the broad rim of his gold-spiked pith helmet, pedaled leisurely along the empty cobblestoned street. The red stripes running down the seams of his black trousers made psychedelic patterns as his polished shoes rotated to propel his bicycle.

I drew back and pulled the draperies together.

The sight of the policeman was sobering.

I found the bathroom and turned on the shower. I

soaped and rinsed myself several times to rid myself of accumulated skin film. But my thoughts kept returning to Karl Erikson incarcerated in a Bahamian jail cell.

I had to talk to Candy Kane.

THREE

I DRIED myself vigorously with a coarse towel, wrapped its dampness around my waist, and went in search of Candy.

Outside the bathroom door I almost ran into Chen Yi, the Chinese girl. It was something of a relief to find that at least her six-foot, four-inch presence had been no dream. She had on another high-necked garment of some gauzy material, barely opaque, but this one reached her ankles. "Good morning," I said. "Or is it afternoon?"

"Early afternoon," she replied. "I've brought you a set of Candy's underwear." She removed it from her arm and handed it to me. I noticed for the first time that despite her size, her voice had a musical, little girl tinkle to it.

"Just what I need," I assured her. "I appreciate it."

She smiled, but her eyes were upon my body above the damp towel fastened at my waist. She made no comment about my body scars, though. "I've pressed your suit for you," she continued.

"That wasn't necessary," I protested halfheartedly. A freshly pressed suit would help a good deal in avoiding attention when I left Candy's. I wondered if Chen Yi had noticed the lack of labels.

I returned to the bathroom with Candy's underwear. His choice ran to bold colors and wild patterns, but the fresh material felt welcome. I went back into the room I had come to think of as the Incense Room and found my freshly shined shoes at one end of the couch with a new pair of socks draped across them. My pressed suit rested on the back of the couch. The hospitality in Candy's apartment almost was embarrassing in its thoroughness.

I pulled on socks and shoes and sat down on the couch opposite the end marked by a slight lumpiness where I had hidden the canvas sack with the papers from the bank's safe deposit boxes. If I followed the script, I'd get to the private airstrip and meet the escape plane. There I'd turn the canvas sack with its contents over to someone named Baker.

I hoped that Baker knew me because I surely didn't know him.

I'd never learned which government agency employed Karl Erikson. There were times when I'd suspected he was a troubleshooter for more than one agency, doing special government jobs on assignment. The only other man who worked with Erikson who was more than a nameless face to me was Jock McLaren. He'd been with Erikson and me on the recovery of an AEC shipment, a job which used an import office on Fifth Avenue in New York City as a cover for the retrieval effort.

But if I left the island now, there was Karl Erikson himself.

Right now he was undoubtedly lodged in the Bahamian equivalent of maximum security. He had made a point of emphasizing, as he always did on these jobs, that we were strictly on our own if anything went wrong. Now that it had, no US consul was about to step around to the Nassau brig and inquire about Karl Erikson's welfare.

No one knew he was there except me.

He had been emphatic about that contingency, too. "If only one of us makes it, there'll be no looking back by the survivor," he'd said to me on the darkened jet which had flown us from Andrews Field when the pilot began to circle the cluster of lights that was Nassau below us in the black water. "The whole purpose is to get what we're after into the right hands."

Which was fine—business as usual—except that I recalled at least twice when he'd violated the rule himself. Once in Cuba he'd come back across an open space he'd successfully traversed to knock out an armed Castro militiaman who was preventing me from taking the same escape route.

And once when he and Hazel and I were in the drink in the south Atlantic after a fishing cruiser had been shot out from under us, he'd tried to save Hazel at a time when he couldn't reasonably have expected to save himself.

I looked up as a sound from a corner of the room caught my attention. Candy Kane was standing in the doorway, his blocky body swathed in a bright purple robe. "Whooo-eee!" he exclaimed with every evidence of deep feeling. "Must've been quite a bash from the way I feel."

"Your brandy is potent," I admitted. He was eyeing my underwear. His underwear. "Chen Yi pressed my suit, too," I added.

He nodded. "The den mother," he said with no particular emphasis. "What'd you think of Hermione?"

"I was trying to make up my mind if I'd dreamed her."

Candy chuckled. "If you'd been goin' to stick around for awhile, I wouldn't have let her tie into you like that. She's shacked up reg'lar with a muscle type, kind of a nasty job when he's turned on. But Hermione enjoys a change of scenery."

"What happens if the muscle type catches her at it?"

"He leans on her, but it's never stopped her yet. I'd have to say the pair of them are well matched." He rubbed his chin. "How long 'd you say last night you wanted to stay?"

"Three or four days. Maybe less." I recalled that Erikson's man Baker was only going to keep the Andrews Field rendezvous for three mornings. "Surely less."

"Seems to me you'd be takin' your fences faster'n that with the bobbies lookin' for you."

"There's a problem. My partner was grabbed last night."

"He was? Where?"

"On the roof of a bank building on Shirley Street."

Candy cocked an eyebrow in a skeptical expression I was beginning to recognize as nearly habitual with him. "You're beginnin' to sound like a real hot potato, Earl. I only get to run my game here on the strength of a couple of contacts an' a little payoff. I can't afford trouble." He moved to the couch and sat down on the other end of it. The papers in the canvas sack crackled slightly under his weight, but he didn't notice. There was a brooding look on his heavy features as his eyes met mine at the closer range. "You know what I mean?"

"Why would anyone look for me here?" I asked in a tone of voice intended to sound reasonable. "There's no possible connection. For the law to suspect, I mean. As for my partner, there's something I'd like to ask you about—"

I broke off as Chen Yi reentered the room. The tall Chinese girl had my washed-and-ironed shirt in her hand. "Thanks again," I said and stood up and began to slip into the shirt.

"What about your partner?" Candy wanted to know. I glanced at the Chinese girl, but Candy waved an impatient hand. "She goes with the lease here. Speak up."

"I'd like to take him with me."

Candy stared. "Take him—? You mean—?"

"It might not be too much of a job, depending upon the detention facilities," I went on. "And I'd pay the right man well for a little help."

"I'm not about to get my black ass fussed up in no jail-break," Candy began, then paused. "You'd pay? For what kind've help?"

"It shouldn't take too much. And I'd expect to pay."

"I could sure use a fresh bankroll," Candy said thoughtfully. "The dice turned real unfriendly since that Las Vegas disaster. Before that I'd been goin' so good you wouldn't believe it." He shrugged. "That's the way it goes. But this thing you're talkin' about—" He was silent for a moment. "Well, how much of a payoff would go to this right man you mentioned?"

I tried to make my tone impressive. "You name it."

He rubbed his chin again. "What kind of help 'd you say?"

"I'd need to know a few things first. Where would he be held?"

"Not at East Street, I wouldn't think," Candy responded immediately. "Cartwright Street more likely. It's kind of an unofficial detention center. Prob'ly not more'n two hundred yards from where you say he was grabbed. Did you score with the bank?"

I knew that my answer would have a lot to do with the price Candy set for his assistance—if he decided to help —and I had no cash to pay off at once. "I'm going to have to come back and retrieve it later when the heat's off," I said.

The answer appeared to satisfy him. "Was there any rough stuff that would make the police hairy?"

I thought of Karl Erikson's thickly thewed body shedding police like pearls from a broken necklace strand. And the wallop I gave the sergeant. "Just a little scuffle on the roof. What kind of a jail is this one you think he'd be in?"

"A bloody poor one, compared to US types," Candy said. "Actually, it's a place people are sometimes held before they appear before a magistrate. I don't think there's more'n half a dozen cells behind the bookin' desk, but even at night there's enough blokes around so no one walks in an' out unless he's got business there."

"Even behind a gun?"

"Don't talk no guns to me, mon. That's out."

"What kind of a building is it?"

"Old like most of the government buildings near Bay Street."

"No, I mean what kind of construction. Masonry? Steel and concrete?"

"Let's see now." Candy's brow furrowed as he tried to remember. "Seems to me it's bricked over now," he said finally, "but when I was a tyke it was a wood-frame-an'-lath affair and old even then. Why?"

"If I can't go in the front, maybe I can go in the back."

"Through the back wall, you mean?"

"Correct." A shaped charge would take care of the wall. Peel it right off like the top of a box of Crackerjack. If I could place such a charge one cell away from Erikson's, he and I would be gone before the startled people in the front of the building had time to notice the brick dust settling on their desks.

"Maybe I should have asked you your reg'lar line of business," Candy said drily. Then he turned serious. "Listen, Earl. What would I have to do? Be right there with you?"

"No," I said. "Just pick up a few things for me ahead of time and furnish transportation for a local run afterward."

"I could really use a bit of financin'," Candy said. He rose to his feet. "Why don't I dress an' go downtown an' make sure he's where I think he is? Then we can haggle when I come back."

"Take a close enough look at the streets around the jail so you can draw me a map," I countered.

Candy slipped an arm around Chen Yi who had been standing silently near the end of the couch. He patted the Chinese girl's right hip. "How about it, luv?" he asked. "Am I daft to get mixed up in this?"

"Not if you aren't actually present," she said in her soft voice. "There can't be many men in this man's situation who would even think about trying to free a captured partner."

"Yeah, but if you'd seen him in action on that cruddy Las Vegas airplane you'd know he cuts more ice than most," Candy returned. "I'll get goin'."

He left the room, and Chen Yi and I were left together. "What would you like to eat?" she asked. "A steak?"

"A steak sounds a bit heavy this early. Scrambled eggs? With bacon?"

"No bacon, but we have sausage."

"Fine."

I completed dressing when Chen Yi went to the kitchen, then took the opportunity afforded by being alone to retrieve the canvas sack from beneath the couch cushion. I hung it around my neck again, flattened it against my chest, and buttoned my jacket carefully so that it didn't show.

I followed Chen Yi into the kitchen which I hadn't seen before. It was well equipped. She had already plugged in a percolater. "How does a girl like you happen to be running a massage parlor in Nassau?" I asked her.

"I was born in Taiwan," she replied, cracking eggs into a blue bowl. "But in 1950 my father, a merchant, had the poor judgment to oppose Chiang Kai-shek's move there. Our family barely escaped."

"And you came here?"

"Not immediately. We lived in Bombay for a time. Then Istanbul, then Vienna. My father was a restless man. I learned the technique of therapy massage in London." She smiled at me from the stove. "Although I seldom get a chance to practice the healing art here. Once in a while a ship's doctor sends me a legitimate customer, usually with arthritis, but the majority of the people I see are expecting something quite different from me."

"I can imagine," I said. "What's Candy's background?"

"He was born here." She brought my eggs and sausage to the table and poured coffee from the percolater. "He is a poor organizer, a poor businessman. He is usually happy to let me manage most of his affairs." Again there was the trace of a smile upon her beautiful face. "So long as I am careful not to give the impression of outright management. His *machismo* will not permit that."

Was she giving me a subtle warning about Candy's unreliability? I began to eat while I considered it. I finally decided it didn't make much difference. Candy might be a rusty tool—and I was only guessing about that—but he was all I had.

I had three cups of coffee, the last one with a dark, tightly rolled cigarette Chen Yi gave me from a box on a shelf. "It's not marijuana," she said when she saw the caution with which I took my first drag. "Just Turkish tobacco. I learned to like—" She paused with her head cocked to one side. "Can that be Candy at the door so soon? He's hardly had time to—"

She didn't complete it but hurried from the kitchen. I heard the sound of the heavy slide bolts being thrown back from the door, and then in what seemed the same instant Candy burst into the kitchen, his black face suffused with emotion. Chen Yi followed a few yards behind him. "Listen, you!" Candy growled at me harshly. "What kind of a mess are you tryin' to get me into?"

"Mess? No mess. I'm just—"

"I'm sure he has no intention—" Chen Yi began in what was obviously intended to be a placating tone of voice.

"Shut up!" Candy barked at her. "You know what this stupid bastard's done? It's all over the island that him an' his crazy partner cracked a box in the bank that was loaded with syndicate papers, that's what! The syndicate's lookin' for this guy twice as hard as the police are!"

"The syndicate controls gambling among the little people," Chen Yi explained, seeing my bewilderment. "Candy, I—"

"I'd run you out've here this second if I wasn't afraid someone'd see you leavin' in daylight an' finger me for keepin' you here," Candy snarled at me. "But as soon as it's dark you're gone! I can't stand no static from those people!"

"I'm sure there's a way it could be handled if—" Chen Yi began again.

"Shut up!" Candy roared. His eyes glittered. "I want him out've here!"

"But I'm sure we could—"

Anger threaded his voice. "I know a bear trap when I see one, woman! They'd close me up in a minute!"

I stacked my dishes and carried them from the table to the sink. I had no desire to be the focal point of a quarrel between these two. Candy was glaring at Chen Yi as though she was the cause of all his problems.

"Candy—" she said quietly.

"SHUT UP!!" It was an outright bellow.

"But if I can explain to you how—"

Candy's voice was suddenly calm when he interrupted her. "Get the cane, Chen Yi."

She appeared surprised. She looked at Candy, glanced at me, then back at Candy. "You will have time for that later. For now you should know—"

"GET THE CANE!"

For an instant I thought she was going to refuse to obey. Then she went behind the kitchen door and took down from a hook a pliant looking cane about twenty-four inches long, the type I'd seen in movies involving British schools. In silence she handed it to Candy. He bent it double upon its own length, testing its flexibility, then gripped its knobby end. "Get your belly down on that table!" he commanded. "That smart mouth of yours will make your ass smart!"

Again I thought she was going to refuse until Chen Yi stretched herself out the long way on the kitchen table. Her beautiful face was an ivory mask. Candy grabbed the trailing edge of her long gown and threw it up onto her back, exposing the long legs, full bare thighs, and splendid nude buttocks. The cane in Candy's hand swished through the air and struck Chen Yi's taut flesh viciously, curling around her seat.

The cane rebounded violently as though rejected by the soft mounds. The Chinese girl's thigh muscles clenched and unclenched, but she made no sound. A long, livid stripe sprang up across her twin globes. I could see a weal rising even before the stripe turned pink, then maroon.

Swhissssshhhhh-crack!

Chen Yi's back arched, but she sank back upon the table top again, still silent.

Swissssshhhhh-crack!

Candy grunted from the effort. "Count, bitch!" he said hoarsely as his arm descended again with the cane a whirring blur at its end.

"Four!" Chen Yi said clearly but in a strangled voice. "How—many?"

"Ten of the best," Candy informed her. Swissssshhhhh-crack! "Count!"

"Five!"

"Six!"

"S-seven!" For the first time there was an audible catch in the Chinese girl's voice as her meaty looking backside was scored again. Rising stripes criss-crossed her bare flesh. Her solid-looking thighs writhed like ivory snakes.

"Eight!" I couldn't understand how Chen Yi kept from screaming until I saw that after each count her mouth went to her arm where she bit herself to subdue her vocal distress.

It was a contest of wills.

Swissssshhhhh-crack!

"N-nine!"

Candy whipped the springy cane down into Chen Yi's multihued twisting mounds with what seemed to be all the strength in his arm.

Swissssshhhhh-CRACK!!

"TEN!!!" It was almost a triumphant shout from Chen Yi.

But Candy raised his arm again.

The Chinese girl came up from the table like a pantheress. Her two hands hooked into Candy, and he went up into the air over her head so effortlessly it was unbelievable. Bright diamond tears glittered at the corners of her eyes but remained unshed. "You said ten!" Chen Yi gritted between clenched teeth.

I expected her to smash Candy to the kitchen floor. Instead, after a three-second pause she lowered him again. "You would have left me no dignity," she said almost in a whisper and left the kitchen without a backward glance. Her gown was still raised high enough on one side for me to see the dark weals standing out on one buttock.

Candy tossed the cane onto the kitchen table. "I've changed my mind!" he snapped at me. "I want you out've here right now, an' I'm not foolin'. An' if you don't believe me, the next time you see me, I'll have a gun in my hand!"

He stalked out, and I was left alone in the kitchen.

The equation had certainly changed.

I didn't believe there was any necessity for Candy's becoming as worked up as he had just shown himself to be even if Erikson and I actually had shoved our noses into syndicate business. Now I had to somehow make myself invisible during the remaining daylight hours before I could return to the airstrip under cover of darkness and sweat out the arrival of the plane in the morning.

Even that presented a problem.

We had touched down at Oakes Field, the island of New Providence's only other landing strip except Nassau's commercial international airport at Windsor Field. Oakes Field was an unlighted, dawn-to-dusk strip supposedly operated solely by and for the membership of the Nassau Flying Club. Erikson had mentioned once that it was through an employee that our spook early morning arrival and departure had been arranged. But I could hardly hang around a private flying field without provoking questions I couldn't answer.

There was one slight advantage. Oakes Field was closer to the downtown area than the international airport. It was within walking distance, actually. If I could just stay undercover during the day, I should be able to walk out to the field at night and deposit myself nearby in a grassy swale to await the plane's arrival.

I turned at a sound from the doorway. I was amazed to see Chen Yi reentering the kitchen. Her tears were gone, and her almost regal, high cheekboned features had regained their usual impassivity. When she reached for the shallow pan of green tea leaves which had been steeping on the back of the stove, her hand trembled, however.

"I apologize for the—the exhibition," she said in a low tone as she poured herself a cup of tea.

"Why do you put up with that sort of thing?" I returned.

She shrugged, smiling faintly. "A woman should be seen and not heard. I provoked him. He had to assert himself." Her dark eyes met mine above the rim of her teacup. "What are you going to do?"

"I've just been debating that."

"It's not only the police who will be looking for you," she said seriously. "There are those who are more to be feared."

"I don't think I really feel—"

Chen Yi was shaking her head, and I stopped. "Candy wouldn't be wrong about syndicate involvement," she said. "Your best hope is to mix with the tourists. If we were on Freeport, I'd suggest taking a guided tour on a bus, but here on our little island we don't have that." She considered for a moment. "There are the surreys," she said at last. "Have you seen them?"

"No, I haven't."

"They are like old-fashioned hansom cabs drawn by a horse. You will find them near any of the beach hotels."

She took a sip of tea. "You have given up the plan to rescue your partner?"

"Certainly for now."

She nodded. "That is wise. I don't think you understand the syndicate situation here in relation to gambling nor the extent to which they can command obedience to their orders. Not from the government, of course, or at least only from a few minor officials. And from only a few of the businessmen, although that is increasing. But from this part of society—" with a sweep of her arm she indicated both the apartment and the area "—they demand and enforce allegiance."

"Where were you educated, Chen Yi?"

"In London, principally." She smiled. "Sometimes it seems like a long time ago."

"I guess I should be leaving before your lord and master comes back to find out why I haven't."

"I wish there were some way I could help you," she said.

"I'll borrow a rabbit's foot if you have one."

"I wish I had one to give you." She turned serious again. "I'll take you downstairs. It's better that you leave from the massage parlor entrance." She led the way toward the barricaded door at the head of the stairs.

I watched her graceful stride. "You're walking well for someone who just about had her tail cut off," I remarked.

"The female behind is a resilient article," Chen Yi said over her shoulder as she threw back the bolt on the door. "Although I'll be sore today, tender tomorrow, and carry the marks for a month." She descended the stairs, and I followed behind her. "This is my place of business."

I stood inside the massage parlor and looked around. The room seemed narrow because of a free-standing wall which divided the space in half. In front of the wall Chen Yi had set up a small office-waiting room equipped with a reception desk, filing cabinet, and a few pieces of lounge furniture.

Four partitioned cubicles were stationed along the back

wall behind the room divider. Each had a canvas curtain hanging from brass rings on a bar across the open front to provide a degree of privacy. I moved to one of the cubicles and pulled the curtain aside. In the center of the enclosure was a sheeted massage table surrounded by heat lamps. Everything was clinically clean. The room had the faint, pleasant odor of rubbing alcohol and wintergreen oil. "How's business?" I asked.

"Steady." She looked significantly at the door.

"Yes," I agreed. "It's about that time. Thanks for all your help."

"I wish I could do more."

"Thanks again," I said and stepped out into the brilliant sunlight that assaulted my eyeballs after the continual artificial lighting at Candy's. I blinked my way up the street, wondering what came next.

I felt as exposed in the hard white light as a freshman girl's pubic hair at a sorority initiation. I was tempted to duck into the first bar I reached, but I passed it up. I knew that bars would be closely checked by both the police and the syndicate, assuming Candy was correct about the syndicate's involvement, although I still found it hard to believe despite Chen Yi's affirmation. My notion of syndicate operation didn't jibe with this tropical locale.

Ahead of me in the next block I saw a father, mother, and two small daughters window shopping. I lengthened my stride to catch up to them and then settled down a few paces behind, close enough so that at a casual glance I could be considered one of the group.

I heard my deliverance before I saw it. Around the next corner came the clop-clop-clop sound of a very slow-moving horse. An ancient surrey appeared, complete to the fringe on top, drawn by an aged mare sheathed in layers of fat. The mare wore a bonnet crowned with pink feathers, giving her a saucy look.

The surrey carried no passengers. I moved out to the curb and raised my hand. The driver didn't see it, but the mare did. She was already slowing down when the driver did a belated double take and began vigorously sawing on the reins. "Yes, sair?" the driver inquired with a wide, beaming, black smile.

"What are your rates?"

"Fo' dollar hour, sair."

"How much for the rest of the afternoon?"

"How fi'teen dollar sound, sair?"

I climbed up into the surrey and handed him fifteen dollars from my thinning roll. "Let's go."

"Yes, sair." Another wide grin. "Someplace special?"

"I want to see it all. Take your time. There's no hurry."

The driver nodded and slapped the reins on the mare's broad rump. "Proceed, Ermintrude," he directed. The mare started up in a swaying canter that rocked the surrey from side to side like a rowboat in a mild cross chop.

The balance of the afternoon was predictable. The driver took me to the usual sightseeing stops and also to all his relatives and friends who had anything to sell. I bought a few small, inexpensive items and stacked the packages on the back seat beside me. There is nothing more touristy than a man with packages. Ermintrude navigated what was evidently a set route by herself while the driver pointed out places of interest to which I paid little attention.

Nassau was small enough so that we soon ran out of the usual tourist attractions. The driver looked at me expectantly. "I'd like to eat," I told him, mindful that I probably wouldn't be eating again until well after daybreak. "Some quiet place."

He took me to a restaurant called Bow Bells on Frederick Street, one of the quieter backwaters of the business district. The sun was sinking, but there was still a good two hours of daylight left. "You like this place good, sair," the driver assured me.

I might well have liked it good if I hadn't had so much

on my mind. I dawdled over the meal, and when I rejoined my transportation, the sudden tropical night wasn't too far distant. "I'd like to see a few of the homes now," I proposed. "The better homes." I already knew that the better homes at this end of the island were in an enclave between Thompson Road and Blue Hill Road. More importantly, so was Oakes Field.

Ermintrude turned into Thompson Road when the driver clucked to her. Five minutes later he stopped by the side of the road while he lighted a lantern which he hung from a hook at the rear of the surrey. Then Ermintrude resumed her steady pace.

The homes on either side of the roadway suggested affluence. It was almost dark, and once back in town there was no reasonable excuse I could use to request the driver to retrace his course to the vicinity of Oakes Field again. I had to make my move now. "This is far enough," I said.

The driver looked around at me in surprise. "Sair?"

I handed him a twenty. "That's a bonus for a good job. It was a pleasant afternoon. I'll stretch my legs now by walking back to town. You can bring the packages to the Anchorage Hotel in the morning. Room 422."

His expression indicated that he didn't like any part of the proposition. "Gentlemon walkin' alone in this neighborhood after dark attract much attention to himself, sair," he suggested delicately.

This district of fine homes was undoubtedly a well-policed area. I could understand it, but I had to buck it. I slid down from the surrey seat and stood by the side of the road. Even Ermintrude turned her head to regard me inquiringly. "I'll be fine," I announced cheerfully. I took hold of Ermintrude's bridle and turned her around in the roadway until she was headed back toward Nassau. "See you in the morning at the hotel," I said and whacked the mare an open-hander across her wide beam. Her eyes rolled at the indignity, and her hooves did a skittish little time step in the road before she got the surrey rolling again.

I stood and watched its bobbing tail light disappear around a corner. I hoped the bonus would keep the driver quiet tonight. Nothing was going to keep him quiet when he tried to deliver the packages to the Anchorage in the morning.

But by that time I wouldn't care.

I hoped.

FOUR

I KNEW approximately where the field was because Erikson and I had hitched a ride to town with the same flying club employee who had agreed to close his eyes to our unauthorized use of it. I walked along the edge of the road in the deepening twilight. The stars were out although the western sky was still pale. The first onset of the night breeze blew gently, and a dog barked occasionally. There was enough scrub brush and foliage just off the roadside that I wasn't concerned about getting myself out of sight in a hurry in case headlights appeared from either direction.

I almost passed Oakes Field without seeing it in the gathering darkness. Only the fact that one asphalt runway extended almost to the road enabled me to spot the darker strip against the green grass. Then I could make out the dim outline of a wire fence. I couldn't see any sign of an adminstration building.

I tried to estimate the direction of a plane's approach in the prevailing wind, then moved in from the road along the fence in a direction that would place me near the touchdown point. A hundred yards off the road I saw the deeper shadow of another runway angling off the first one, shattering my hope that I could predict accurately where the plane would land.

I burrowed down into the waist-deep grass alongside the

fence at a point near the junction of the runways and prepared to try for a little sleep before sweating out the final hours before dawn. I didn't get any real sleep, but I dozed off from time to time. Once I woke myself by rolling over in the grass and striking my hand against the chain link fence. I couldn't see my watch, but there was no feel of dawn in the air.

I tried to shift to a more comfortable position, and the papers inside the canvas sack still suspended from my neck crackled noisily, reminding me why I was there. I thought of Karl Erikson trying to sleep in whatever cell the Bahamas police force had lodged him in.

I became aware that my gaze had fixed itself upon a pair of headlights slowly circling the perimeter road outside the fence bordering the airport. A night watchman? The police? The cruising car didn't come near enough to where I lay next to the fence for me to make an identification, and I wasn't about to leave my comparatively safe haven to satisfy my curiosity.

When I saw the headlights a second time twenty minutes later in the same deliberate pattern through the area, I was sure it was the police. If a manhunt were actually underway, it would be poor police tactics if one of the prime escape areas on the island—even if an unlikely one in their estimation—went unpatrolled.

It changed my thinking about my own tactics. I had planned on remaining outside the fence until Erikson's pickup plane actually arrived. Now I couldn't afford that luxury if the police remained as active as they gave every indication of being.

During an interval when the cruising headlights were absent, I knelt in the grass and made a shield of my jacket while I risked striking a match to take a quick look at my watch. It was 3:35 A.M. There was still no light in the sky, but a change in the quality of the darkness promised that the first light streaks of dawn would be evident before too much longer.

I rose to my feet and removed my jacket and the canvas sack from around my neck. I pitched both over the fence, then clawed and toed my way to the top of the swaying, eight-foot barrier, and jumped down. I landed in soft sand next to a palmetto bush. Only the whispering rustle of palm fronds disturbed by the salt breeze intruded upon the silence.

I recovered the jacket and sack and made my way in the loose, clinging sand bordering a runway. I judged the plane would roll to a stop at the end of the strip if the diminishing wind continued to blow from its present direction. Then I stretched out in the sand with the straggling palmetto bushes screening me from the road. The cover wasn't as good as it had been outside the fence, but my ability to move rapidly had increased vastly.

The patrolling car—if in fact it was the same one—made one more pass along the perimeter road before fingers of light in the eastern sky alerted me to the advent of action. The plane was supposed to land as soon after dawn as the pilot's judgment permitted.

The air grew cooler as the breeze seemed to fade even more. A faint odor of decaying seaweed was carried on the light eddies of air which now seemed to be on my left cheek instead of fullface as before, although they weren't strong enough for me to be sure.

I replaced the canvas sack around my neck and re-buttoned my jacket. I would need both hands free to scramble into the escape aircraft with a minimum of delay. The gradual infiltration of light upon the field had grown sufficiently for me to make out the dark bulk of the field's administration building to one side of the longest runway. I could see no activity there.

The increasing light also disclosed that the asphalt strips branching off from the principal runway formed a pattern shaped like the letter K. I wondered again if I had selected the correct place to position myself. Conceivably, the pickup plane could land on any of the strips, depending upon surface wind direction. There was nothing I could do except wait and see.

The light had increased to a point where I began to think something had thrown off the planned rendezvous. It seemed to me there was more than adequate light for a plane to land. Then from the direction of the water I heard the distant whine of turbine engines.

A plane flashed low overhead, a golden streak in the first rays of the sun. It pitched up into a steep climbing turn, dropping wheels and flaps in an acrobatic, unorthodox maneuver. It was going to be on the ground before anyone realized it was there. I stood up and waited. I still couldn't tell which landing strip the pilot intended to use. There was practically no wind at all.

Only when the plane leveled out low in its final glide did I see that it was going to end up at the opposite end of the runway where I had stationed myself. I began to run through loose, damp sand that grabbed at my feet and seeped into my low-cut shoes. The crucifix of the plane hurtled past me, and I heard the screech of tortured tires biting into the asphalt. I swerved onto the runway into an invisible cloud of heat and kerosene fumes, but the better footing permitted me to run faster.

I couldn't understand why the sound of the jet engines seemed to intensify until I realized I was hearing a second plane. I skidded to a stop on the asphalt. My pursuit of the rescuing jet had brought me almost midpoint of the long runway where the auxiliary strips intersected it, and to my left another aircraft, a single-engine piston type was in its final landing pattern and headed almost right for me.

I had to wait until it touched down and rolled rapidly toward the administration building. I could see heads looking out the side windows of the second plane. I began to run again as a door above the wing of the second plane opened and two women and a man clambered out, followed by a second man who stood on the wing and

looked long and hard at the squatty jet at the farthest end
of the main runway. A Bahamian businessman home
from an all-night party at one of the Out Islands, I decided,
and wondering what the strange plane was doing at this
private field.

My breath was coming harder as I tried to increase my
speed. The runway seemed endless. The man jumped
down from the wing of the plane and began to walk
quickly toward the jet. His course roughly paralleled my
own. He began to run, too, trying to cut me off.

The pickup plane loomed close at hand now, though. I
could see movement through its oval windows in the side
of the smooth, cylindrical fuselage. Then the door which
fit so snugly it was barely discernible was drawn inward.
There were no markings on the plane at all.

A light-haired man in a brilliant orange flying suit appeared in the opening. A glance to the side revealed that
the pilot of the private plane had unaccountably stopped
running. He was staring at a corner of the field where a car
I hadn't noticed before was parked against the wire fence.
Three dark figures were scrambling over its chain link
barrier.

I raced around the rescuing plane's jutting wingtip and
hurled myself through the open door, almost knocking
the man in the orange flying suit off his feet. "One
pigeon in the roost, Artie," he yelled up to the pilot,
whom I could see with earphones cocked on his head so
that one ear was exposed.

"Just—me," I gasped. "Move—out—here!"

"Pappy said there'd be two of you," the copilot said in a
doubtful tone.

"No!" I got out with as much volume as I could muster.
"Get—rolling!"

"Bumblebees outside, Sam," the pilot drawled from
up forward. "Batten hatches."

I lurched to my feet as the sandyhaired copilot pulled
the opened door shut and threw over the locking lever.

Through one of the oval windows I could see the three men who had climbed the fence were halfway across the field. Their right arms were extended and dots of winking yellow light appeared at the ends of them.

"Pour it on, skipper!" the copilot shouted. "The uglies have arrived!"

The plane surged forward, and the copilot grabbed at the back of a cushioned seat as the cabin swerved with the unlocking of brakes. "Grab yourself a pad and buckle in," he called to me over his shoulder as he strained against the increasing acceleration to make his way to the cockpit.

We were really rolling by the time I clamped a seat belt across my middle. I had a quick glimpse of the private pilot flat on the ground, dodging bullets. Just beyond him on the perimeter road a jeep was making the scene.

I was pretty sure police were in the jeep.

Police wouldn't charge across an airstrip shooting at an unidentified plane.

So Candy had been right in his insistence that syndicate toes had been tramped on.

Our plane banked until its silvered wing glistened in the sunlight. Far below I could see tiny figures in positions which indicated the three assailants had reversed direction and were running toward the fence and their car.

Then we were out over the water, and I couldn't see Oakes Field at all.

The force of the acceleration as the plane continued to angle upward forced me back into the deep cushioned seat. In the aftermath I felt dead beat but too keyed up to relax. Candy's sudden change of attitude had been baffling, and I hadn't really believed his seeming near terror was justified until I saw the assault wave coming at me over the airport fence. I'd always felt that Candy had steel cables for nerves, and his loudly expressed angry fear had seemed a rank overstatement of the seriousness of the situation until the close call a few moments before had proven him right.

Thinking back, I had to wonder if I hadn't inadvertently blocked all escape routes for Erikson. I hadn't mentioned his name, but both Chen Yi and Candy knew I had a partner in police hands. Candy knew it had something to do with a bank.

I had spoken too freely in Candy's apartment when I was thinking only in terms of the police. I was certain that none of the group on Eurydice Street would run to the police with information, but the syndicate was another matter. Hadn't Candy remarked that Hermione was a gangster's girl friend? I wished I knew exactly what I'd said during that brandy-filled night when I felt fairly secure.

If Candy or Chen Yi talked under syndicate pressure, I had made Erikson a syndicate target.

It was a thought I didn't like.

I reached down for the seat lever to incline the seat back. Just as I touched it, an alarm bell sounded in the cockpit, and a red light flashed on above my head. An emergency oxygen mask dropped down and dangled in front of my face. I grabbed for it and then was thrown forward as the pilot suddenly pulled back the throttles and abruptly leveled the plane from what been a steady climb.

The copilot scrambled back into the cabin, a flashlight in his hand. "Don't crap your pants yet, Mac," he advised me. "We've lost cabin pressure, that's all. You won't need that mask unless the skipper decides to go higher to get above a storm ahead of us. Meanwhile I'll check the door seal and latch."

I turned to watch him as he brushed past me. I wondered if parachutes were concealed somewhere in the aircraft's plush interior. The copilot bent close to the fuselage door, then swung open a smaller door at the rear of the cabin. Apparently finding nothing there, he reversed direction and started back up the aisle.

He stopped partway and pushed the flat of his hand against the cream-colored vinyl overhead. Two small perforations marred the smooth interior. He probed with a finger, then inserted it into the break and ripped away the outer fabric. He pulled thick, soundproof padding away until the bare metal skin of the fuselage was exposed. "Damn!" he exclaimed. "We've been holed!"

I could see twin punch-outs the size of thimbles about four inches apart. The copilot spun around and stared at the plane's opposite side. Two ragged slits showed in the vinyl, and when he peeled the soundproofing away, two much larger rents in the metal were exposed, made by tumbling bullets during their exit.

"Is it bad?" I asked. I hoped my voice didn't reveal the totality of my concern.

My question fell unheeded upon the copilot's retreating back. Through the open cockpit door I could see him consulting with the pilot, who advanced the throttles again. I noticed, though, that he kept the plane in level flight.

The copilot returned and shoved dangling oxygen masks above each empty passenger seat back into overhead compartments. I fumbled with mine until he took over impatiently. "There's nothing to worry about," he said. "This little fat cat will hold together through a lot worse than this, but the bullet holes will keep us from flying above ten thousand feet. Safety regulations prohibit it."

His tone was accusing, as if I were responsible for the plane damage. And in a way I guess I was. "So we'll hold at nine thousand, and that means we won't get you back on schedule," he continued. "At that altitude we'll have turbulence and head winds because of the storm I mentioned. We'd planned to top it at thirty-eight thousand feet, but now we can't. We'll use twice as much fuel at the lower level, so we'll radio ahead for a clearance into Patrick Air Force Base for refueling and quick repairs."

"Can the condition get any worse?"

"Only if one of our wingtip fuel tanks was holed, and there hasn't been any indication of it on the fuel gauges. All it would mean anyway is that Patrick would be the end of the line for you on this flying carpet. You'd have to contact your office and make other travel arrangements." He returned to the cockpit.

I had a mental picture of myself trying to call my office and make other travel arrangements. I knew no office to call. Erikson had always handled all that. These jet jockeys might not know it, but they had a passenger until they landed me at Andrews, no matter how long it took.

But I could see another problem on the horizon. A slow flight and a stop at Patrick AFB meant I was going to be late for the 8:00 A.M. rendezvous with Erikson's man Baker who was to be at Andrews only for ten minute intervals each twenty-four hours. What was I going to do with myself for twenty-four hours while I waited for the next rendezvous interval?

I put it out of my mind. Moments later I fell asleep. Or rather I dozed. I kept being wakened by the pitching of the plane. Over the steady hum of the engines I could hear a new, drumming sound. When I looked out the window, I could see heavy rain blasting against the fuselage. Driblets of water came through the bullet holes overhead. Once a lightning flash so bright it pierced my closed eyelids brought me to full consciousness with a start, but soon I went back to sleep again.

I was awakened fully by the thump of our landing. In contrast to the brilliant sunrise of our takeoff it was a dark gray morning. The plane rolled along a rain-slicked runway and turned off at its end. We bobbed and lurched along for a short distance, then swung onto a hardstand shielded on three sides by high earthern embankments. The plane spun around and stopped. A fuel truck halted alongside with a hiss of air brakes. "This shouldn't take long," the pilot said to me as he left the cockpit.

A sunburned mechanic entered the plane when the door

was opened. He carried a tool box. He and a companion began hammering and pounding inside the plane and out, creating an unholy, ear splitting racket as they anchored temporary metal patches to the bullet-torn fuselage. It didn't take them long, and I looked out to see the fuel hose being snaked back aboard the truck. Everyone worked with the speed and precision of a Daytona Speedway pit crew. Not that it made that much difference, since the time we'd lost flying at low altitude and bucking the storm had already made me miss the Andrews Field rendezvous for that morning.

Within minutes we were back in the air, climbing rapidly as we paralleled the east coast of Florida. The sky lightened as we gained altitude. I became conscious of a tugging at my sleeve; I had fallen asleep again. I couldn't seem to get rested.

The copilot was placing a briefcase in my lap. "We'll be letting down shortly," he said. "My instructions were to give you these." He flicked a hand at the briefcase— an attaché case type—and then handed me two keys. He hesitated a moment before continuing. "Sorry about your buddy," he said awkwardly. "I wouldn't have your job for four times the pay." He went back to the cockpit.

I found that each briefcase latch had its own lock, which accounted for the two keys. After some fumbling I discovered that a half-turn of one key in the left-hand lock released a pin that permitted the right-hand lock to be opened with the other key. Only after that could the left-hand lock be sprung. Erikson had evidently planned for each of us to have a key to this briefcase, which afforded security by ordinarily requiring two individuals to open it.

I propped up the attaché case lid and looked inside. The case held nothing but two plastic cards which were strung individually on metal bead chains. The faces of the cards appeared blank except for an intricate network of threadlike wires imbedded under the slick coating. The letter *Q* was imprinted on the back of each card and beneath that a nine-digit identification number. The beaded chains were to permit the cards to be worn around the neck. There had evidently been one for Erikson and one for me. Where and when I would use mine was still a mystery.

The briefcase itself had obviously been provided as a receptacle for the material we had obtained from the bank. I transferred the contents of the canvas sack to the briefcase and for the first time had a look at the material the sack had contained. Most of it was loose papers, some so old they had become discolored with age.

There was a half-inch-thick pack of ledger sheets, but the only entries I could understand were the figures. It wasn't English. I guessed it was either Spanish or Italian. And the figures were written with a European slant including the characteristic short bar drawn through the upright stroke of the 7s.

One thing I couldn't overlook was the amount column at the right-hand side of the ledger sheets. Few had less than eight digits. Even if the figures represented lira or Swiss or French francs, it was a cinch the carefully preserved records represented some kind of financial dealings in the millions of dollars.

I looked at the rest of the material quickly. Flat cardboard boxes contained reels of film. A few single negatives I held up to the light disclosed groups of men. And there were half a dozen slim, leather-bound, diary-type books in which the writing again was not in English.

I found pages of Italian names while leafing through one of these. In parentheses behind the names were listings such as Banc de Suisse, Banque du Martinique, and Banca la Roma. Letters and numbers following the listings evidently represented some sort of identification, and these in turn were followed by more of the eight and nine digit numbers I'd seen before. It didn't take a giant intellect to perceive that I was looking at a record of secret bank accounts.

Ever since the semicommando assault wave at Oakes Field, I'd had a growing suspicion what Erikson had been after inside the safe deposit boxes we'd rifled. Now I knew for sure. I closed and carefully locked the briefcase with its incriminating material. The innocent-looking briefcase contained a time bomb for someone or a lot of someones. All I wanted to do was get rid of the thing.

I should have paid more attention to Candy. He was on his home turf and certainly should have known the score, but it just hadn't sounded reasonable. Unknowingly, I might have put Candy on a tough spot. The syndicate had a long arm, and if they backtracked to Candy, they might backtrack to Erikson. I didn't like what I was thinking. I wanted to tell my story to someone who could set the wheels in motion to jerk Karl Erikson the hell out of Nassau.

We had been flying in bright sunshine which reflected dazzlingly at times from the wing outside my window. Then the light was obscured as the plane entered a thick cloud bank. It took me a second to realize that we had started descending. A series of squeaks, squeals, and whistles filled the cabin, and the light outside grew more dim.

A gray strip of concrete appeared below us, and the plane eased down upon it so smoothly I didn't know when the wheels made contact. A low layer of fog capped the field, explaining the semidarkness of the descent. A blur of unfamiliar buildings flowed by my window. These were abruptly blocked out by lines of aircraft all bearing USAF insignia. Then in an open space between the planes there appeared a low, squat building with a sign that said Andrews Air Force Base Operations.

I'd landed at the huge military airfield near Washington, D.C., once before on a job with Erikson. Our plane turned onto a taxi strip that led away from the populated area. It rumbled and rolled along for what seemed miles and eventually turned off onto a concrete road that cut between a screen of tall pine trees.

Still the plane kept taxiing. A quarter mile farther on we entered a vast concrete-ramp area in front of four tremendous hangars. All around the parking area was a collection of strange-looking aircraft. I recognized U-2 spy planes wearing dull black paint, their long, narrow, drooping wings held up from the ground by outrigger wheels at their wingtips.

Some planes I didn't recognize. There was a four-engine turboprop transport painted a pale sky blue. A low, squatty, single-seat fighter plane was tucked under one wing of the transport. The fighter had splashes of green, brown, and yellow paint intermixed in such a way its outline could barely be distinguished against the verdant pine tree background. Like the jet that had brought me here none of the aircraft bore identifying marks of any kind.

Helicopters and reconnaissance planes were jammed together nearby. In front of each plane was stationed an armed guard. Everything in sight looked perfectly capable of taking part in a Skunk Works' Department of Dirty Tricks operation. I had never know about this area at Andrews before, and I wondered how many people actually did know about this separate installation at one of the country's busiest military airfields.

A canopied, flatbed trailer towed by a slow-moving tractor approached us. Mechanics wearing white coveralls devoid of any indication of service or rank dropped off the trailer. One herded our plane into a vacant spot with hand signals. When the engines whined to a stop, the two pilots stepped aside to let me precede them out the opened door. I noticed that around their necks they were wearing plastic cards on beaded chains similar to the ones I'd found in the briefcase, and I put one on, too.

I ducked under the plane's wing short of the streamlined fuel pod at its tip to avoid being run over by the inevitable fuel bowser pulling into position alongside. The pilots followed, one carrying a bulging navigation kit. They seemed ready to walk off and forget me. "What do I do now?" I asked.

Both men looked at me in surprise, then the pilot spoke with seeming understanding. "We got you in here late, you know. Your contact probably figured you weren't going to make it today and left. You'll have to call your office. Our job is finished, and we've got to check in. It's been a long day."

"Night," the copilot corrected him.

"I'll go with you," I suggested.

The pilot tapped the red Q on the plastic card on my chest, then pointed to his own which had a green Omega symbol. "You couldn't get within twenty yards of the Omega compound with that badge," he said. He sounded suspicious, as though I were trying to put something over on him. "The only thing a Q card will get you around here is a one-way trip out the gate."

Pilot and copilot walked away from me. As I stared after them, I was asked to move by a mechanic trailing a fuel hose. After the pilots' warning I didn't attempt to follow them. Confronting me in the opposite direction was a regular obstacle course of sober-faced guards.

I cruised through the area letting the position of the guards plot my course. I ended up going down a sidewalk to the right of the hangar line. At its end stood a gatehouse hemmed in on either side by double chain link fences with an electronic alarm system located in the eight-foot deadman's area between the fences.

Outside the gatehouse I could see a street and a large parking lot beyond it. I slowed down and watched the procedure followed by men coming from the parking lot into the area where I was. Each one as he approached the gate took the plastic card looped on the chain around his neck and lifted it chin-high to insert it into a slot anchored to a six-foot-high, steel-barred turnstile.

The men who carried lunch pails placed them in an open-end box imbedded in the gate house wall and left them there until a light above the inspection box turned green. Only after having passed both lunch inspection and establishment of his bona fides with his coded card did the turnstile click open and permit the man to enter.

Once clued, I could see that an identical arrangement was set up for the exit side. I walked to the turnstile, stuck my plastic card into the slot, and laid the briefcase in the inspection compartment. The light turned green, but the turnstile remained locked. I pushed on the horizontal bars, but they wouldn't yield.

In the midst of my struggle with the turnstile I became aware that a guard was watching me. He strolled toward me when he saw I couldn't open the gate. "Leave the card in the slot and step back," he ordered crisply.

I ducked my head out from under the beaded chain and took three paces to the rear. When the guard saw I was clear of the gate, he pulled my card out of the slot, looked at it, turned it over, and reinserted it. The turnstile latch clicked. The guard looked at me pityingly as he would at an idiot child. "Okay," he said gruffly.

I reached for the edge of the card that projected from the slot as I approached the turnstile again. My hand closed upon it but the card stuck fast. I pulled harder. My fingers slipped from its slick surface.

The guard was frowning. "It won't release until you've passed through," he said. "It's a one-way pass. Exit only. It's designed so we can't fail to pick them up. The gate will release it after you pass through the turnstile, and I'll send it on to your security section."

I stopped with a hand on the turnstile. A one-way pass? That's what the pilot had said, too. "Listen, I've got to get back in here," I said.

"Not with that badge, man," the guard said emphatically. "That's a passout only."

I began to sweat. Once through the gate how was I going to get back inside to keep the rendezvous with Erikson's man, Baker? From the looks of this place they weren't about to let me hang around inside the place either. For a second I thought I had an out: I had Erikson's badge in the briefcase, but then that faint hope faded when I remembered that his badge was identical to mine and was one-way, too. If he had been with me, there'd have been no problem, but now I didn't know what to do.

The guard was looking me over closely. "Buddy, get moving, or I'll enforce section twelve of the new regs and detain you as a suspicious character. What are you trying to pull on me? Are you one of these security guys with your pretend-you-don't-know-the-procedures gimmick? Go on, get lost. Maybe I ought to run you in anyway. I could use a commendation in my file."

I could let him run me in, but what then? Nobody knew Erikson's business except Erikson's bosses, and how was I supposed to get in touch with them? And if I let anyone not in the know separate me from the briefcase and its contents, how was I going to interest anyone in Karl Erikson's plight?

The guard took a step toward me, and reflex took over. I went through the turnstile like a seed squeezed from a slice of lemon. If I didn't get out of there, the first thing I knew, I'd be trying to answer FBI questions with no government agency security umbrella in the present and a whole lifetime of unwhitewashed activities in the past.

I reached the street with the guard's eyes boring a hole in my back. I looked at the acres of cars in the lot across the street. I hadn't stolen a car in years, but it looked like my only way of getting away from this birdcage.

And then along came salvation.

A taxi pulled up in front of the gate to permit a distinguished gray-haired man in a business suit to alight. I was in the back seat before the driver could produce change for his fare.

The cabbie looked over his shoulder at me. "Where to?"

I drew a deep breath. "Downtown Washington. I'll tell you where later."

I needed time to think.

FIVE

I WAS in such a mental turmoil at the frustration in not being allowed to make the necessary contact with Erikson's man that the cab was already crossing over the Fourteenth Street Bridge when I looked out the window. The fog had thinned, but it was still a gloomy day.

I still had no idea where to go to get rid of the briefcase.

I leaned back in the cab and tried to think of everything that Erikson had said when he showed up at Hazel's ranch. I tried to recall something in his conversation that would give me a clue as to which government agency might have commissioned his trip to Nassau, however unofficially.

But I couldn't think of a thing.

The more I puzzled over it, the more endless the possibilities became. The Central Intelligence Agency certainly couldn't be excluded, even though the affair seemed to be taking on the dimensions of a police case rather than a matter of national security. One factor pointing to the CIA was the fact that the fishing-in-troubled-waters expedition had taken place outside the continental US, where I assumed the CIA had prime control.

I had heard Erikson state that the National Security Agency operated almost entirely in the communications-intelligence field with few overt acts, so it was unlikely to be them. The FBI hardly seemed a better possibility for two reasons: (1) I knew they jealously worked alone unless conditions were imposed upon them from the top, and (2) their fiefdom was the forty-eight plus two with British-influenced Nassau outside their bailiwick.

Experience gained from working with Erikson in the past wasn't much help in making up my mind either. When we were in Cuba together, the Treasury Department had assigned him the task of recovering a wad of cash sent there years before by the State Department but since disowned by it as a political hot potato. Both departments had taken a more than casual interest in our eventual retrieval of the cash.

The Atomic Energy Commission had been the agency of prime concern when we stopped an unwholesome type at the UN who all but had his hands on a nuclear weapons core being shipped across the country. The Department of Defense also looked over our shoulders on that one.

The present situation had overtones of the Treasury Department again since it appeared that income tax evasion could be involved, but it could also be the Justice Department or one of the myriad smaller agencies recently established by Congress to crack down upon organized crime.

I was struck by another thought. Even if I did learn which agency had sent Erikson to Nevada to recruit me for the safe deposit box job in Nassau, I probably wasn't in much better shape. No matter which government department was involved, Erikson wouldn't have been commissioned by a man sitting in an open office for the world to see. Far more likely the man would be layers deep in the internal structure of his organization, hidden away in an office that never saw daylight.

The cab driver turned on the front seat and looked over his shoulder. We were approaching Constitution Avenue with the Washington Memorial on the left. I still didn't know where to tell the cabbie to take me. Go left to the

Navy Department building and try to get a line on Erikson's boss via the Bureau of Personnel? Turn right and see if I could do any good at the Justice Department? Or go straight ahead to the Treasury Department on Pennsylvania Avenue since I knew one of Erikson's jobs had originated there and this one seemed a possible?

"Where to, mister?" the cabbie said when a red light halted us.

I didn't answer him.

Erikson's only contact I'd actually met and was able to put a name to was Jock McLaren, a specialist who worked for Erikson out of a supposed export-import office on Fifth Avenue in New York City. If I could reach him, Jock McLaren might be able to steer me in the right direction. He should also have a real concern for Erikson's present predicament. The trouble was that the Fifth Avenue office had an unlisted phone, and I didn't know the number.

The cab driver turned squarely around in the front seat. "You did mean Washington, D.C.?" he demanded sarcastically. "Or maybe you had in mind Seattle, Washington?"

"How did the nightclub circuit ever miss a comedian like you?" I countered somewhat weakly. "You can let me out right here."

The cab crossed Constitution Avenue and pulled in to the curb. "I ain't got time to count my buttons while you flyboys try to make up your mind which broad you're gonna shack up with tonight," the driver grumbled.

I paid him and got out of the cab, clutching the briefcase. "You don't want to make us flyboys mad," I told him, "or the next time we're up there in a C-5A, we'll buzz your house and roll our landing wheels up your roof."

He grunted something unintelligible and pulled away.

I waited for the light to change, crossed the street, and began flagging taxis headed the other way. Most were occupied, but I finally caught an empty. "National Airport," I said as I climbed into the back seat. Even if it hadn't been instinctive not to let the original cabbie take me from Andrews' back door to National, I'd have felt like a fool telling the first one to take me back to a point just around the corner from where I'd started.

I was impatient now that I'd finally decided what to do. At the airport I went directly to the Eastern shuttle window and got myself ticketed. I only had to wait twenty minutes before boarding the next plane to New York. While awaiting takeoff, I amused myself—except that amused wasn't precisely the word—by counting my diminishing bankroll. It was under five hundred dollars, and if I were the nervous type, I'd have been nervous. To me money means maneuverability, and very shortly I was due to have my options cut.

The eighty-minute flight to New York was uneventful. I took the airport bus to the East Side Terminal and then caught a cab to 505 Fifth Avenue. I almost fell asleep in the cab. During the past seventy-two hours I'd had a few brandy-fumed hours of sleep at Candy's, a few uneasy catnaps in the grass outside the fence at Oakes Field, and a few half-awake, half-asleep moments on the flight from Nassau to Washington. Otherwise I'd been on the go almost constantly.

The small lobby at 505 Fifth Avenue was deserted as usual. The last time I was there I'd been afraid I was followed, and I'd waited in a corner of the lobby to see if anyone followed me inside from the street. This time it wasn't a problem. I took the elevator to the fifteenth floor.

When I stepped out into the corridor, even before the hum of the elevator faded from my ears, I could see that it wasn't business as usual at the office I'd come to visit. That particular door in a long line of frosted-glass doors stood open, and the corridor walls on both sides were lined with heavy steel-strapped crates, leaving only a narrow passage between.

I walked to the open door. There was no one at the desk in the tiny receptionist's office. I looked inside the office that had been Karl Erikson's. There was no one there, either. The large picture on the far wall which had served to conceal the entrance to a hidden room was gone.

The entrance stood open, and inside I could see more crates. Some were packed, and some in the process of being packed. I was sure they contained the closed circuit television sets, tape recorders, listening devices, snooperscopes, guerrilla-type weapons, and other sophisticated equipment we had found so useful. Now they evidently were being shipped out.

The thought of the weapons supply in the formerly hidden room made my mouth water. My own gun was at the bottom of the elevator shaft in the Nassau bank building where Erikson had deliberately dropped it. Certainly Erikson owed me a replacement, and here was a chance to help him fill that obligation without my getting tangled up in logistical red tape.

I walked into the hidden room. There were only four crates that already had tops screwed onto them. I dug around in the open ones. The first contained various types of microphones; a second smaller one, an assortment of bumper beepers carefully packed in crushproof cartons. But the third held an eyepopping assortment of Beretta .22s, Walther .38s, and Smith & Wesson .38 police specials.

I grabbed an S&W .38, hefted it, then dropped it into my pocket. My shoulder holster was a tightly rolled lightweight bulge inside my jacket. I was so used to wearing a .38 on my left side that I'd felt lopsided ever since losing it. I found ammunition in the bottom of the crate, and I took a box.

I had already started out of the hidden room when I heard the sound of a door being closed across the hall. I reached the entrance between Erikson's former office and the receptionist's cubbyhole at the same time a short, roundish man with a pepper-and-salt crewcut bustled through the corridor door. He stopped short at the sight of me. "This is a private office," he said sharply. His glance lingered briefly on the attaché case in my hand. "Do you have business here, sir?" He looked and sounded like an office manager.

"I'd like to see Jock McLaren," I told him.

"Never heard of him," the roundish man replied.

It could have been true, but I didn't believe it was true. "He worked out of this office," I tried again. "Sandy-haired, youngish, very good with locks."

"Locks?"

I started to heat up at what I felt sure was deliberate evasion. "Locks," I repeated. "And at getting into unopened envelopes with knitting needles. And fluoroscoping envelopes to detect trigger mechanisms inside. Recognize him now?"

"No."

"He worked for Karl Erikson," I continued doggedly.

"I went to school with a Tom Ericksen," the roundish man offered. He smirked in what might have been intended as a smile. "But I don't suppose it's the same one." I took a step toward him, and he backed away, an expression of alarm on his puffy face. "Here now!" he blustered. "I'm only trying to help!" His gaze again lingered momentarily on the briefcase in my hand.

"Like hell you're trying to help!" I unloaded on him. "There's probably some sort of password or code word necessary to crack the magic circle around here, but I don't have it. All I want to do is talk to Jock McLaren."

"Sorry," my opponent said curtly. He appeared to be regaining his courage now that I'd stopped my advance upon him.

"Sorry he's not here or sorry you won't let me talk to him?" I persisted.

There was no reply. I shoved the briefcase toward the roundish man. "Recognize that?" I demanded.

"Certainly," he replied so promptly that it surprised me. "It's a type 27 courier case. But it hasn't been used for some time, although we used to—" His lips closed suddenly in a firm cautionary line. "And anyway I have no authority to—" He let that sentence trail off, too.

I realized I was up against a dead end. This was no field operative. This was some minor bureaucrat charged with inventorying and cleaning out an address no longer in use. He might or might not know Jock McLaren, but if Jock McLaren had already been transferred, this man certainly wouldn't know where. He worked with pencil and paper, not with damn fools like me carrying a briefcase loaded with financial dynamite.

I wondered if he'd try to give me a hard time about getting out of the place considering my unauthorized entrance. I took another deliberate step toward him. He jumped to one side, then backed away, obviously fearful of the uncouth type I represented. He made no move to stop me as I made my way past him. I traversed the narrow passage afforded by the double row of crates in the corridor and took the elevator down to the street.

I had some more thinking to do, but it was going to have to wait. I felt numb from the brick walls I'd been butting with my head. What I needed was sleep. A side street hotel that wouldn't question only a briefcase for luggage would do nicely.

I found one and was assigned a room for four dollars. There was no bellboy. I went upstairs alone, checked the floor for cockroaches and the bed for bugs, found neither, wedged the room's only chair under the doorknob after locking the door, put the briefcase under the mattress at the foot of the bed, stripped, and piled in.

My last conscious thought was a wish for a better day on the morrow. There were still a few hours left in the current day, but my only use for them was to recharge my rundown batteries.

When I opened my eyes, my watch announced I'd been asleep for fifteen hours. Early morning sunlight was streaming in a window. I dressed quickly after dashing water on my face from a wash basin in a corner of the room. Once again I was thankful that a beard is no problem for me. Not that I'd recommend to anyone the route I took to achieve a beardless state.

I retrieved the briefcase from under the mattress at the foot of the bed, then sat down upon the bed's edge to collect my scattered thoughts. Whatever had been marinating in my subconscious during the night, one idea had floated to the surface: I had blown a beautiful chance to get rid of the briefcase yesterday when I was in Erikson's old office amidst the open crates.

If I hadn't been so intent upon rearming myself, I could have stuffed the briefcase inside one of the crates, covered it with a few handfuls of the loose packing excelsior lying around, and left it to be delivered wherever the shipment was going. When the crates were eventually opened and the contents checked against the waybills, someone would discover the extra item.

Security men would first check it out with fluoroscopes, sonic probes, and other electronic devices, but sooner or later it would be opened and—hopefully—turned over to someone who would know what to do with it, since Karl Erikson had been connected with that office. Or was that asking too much of the Washington muddle boys? At any rate I'd missed the chance.

I wondered suddenly if it was too late. They hadn't finished packing the crates yesterday. If they were still at it today, I might be able to get rid of the briefcase after all. I'd have to talk my way past the office-manager-type somehow, but I'd worry about that bridge when I came to it.

I jerked the chair out from under the doorknob and

opened the door. Directly across the hall the door was also open, and a two-hundred pound female with a baby-doll face reposed naked on a double bed. She had a box of chocolates resting on the plateau between her huge breasts and bulbous stomach. "C'mon in, honey," she said to me. I went down the corridor to the wheezing elevator, wondering if I'd be kicking myself when I was old and gray at such missed opportunities.

I walked the short distance to the Fifth Avenue office. The second I stepped off the fifteenth floor elevator I knew my luck was no better today than it had been yesterday. The crates that had lined the corridor were gone. Why the hell hadn't I had the idea yesterday when I could have done something about it?

I stopped near the elevator when I saw the crates had disappeared. The door of Erikson's former office was open again, and I could hear someone moving around inside. I went to the door and looked in. A stoop-shouldered janitor wearing a three-day growth of beard and a frazzled yachting cap was pushing a long-handled broom around the cardboard scraps and excelsior waste on the floor.

"Nobody here," the janitor informed me needlessly when he saw me in the doorway.

"I'm just checking out the office," I said.

"If you wanna rent, you gotta see the building super," he said. He scooped up a nest of assorted trash and dumped it into a large bin resting on a wooden frame equipped with swivel caster wheels.

Projecting from a corner of the movable trash bin was a segment of brown, stiff, oily paper smeared with black paint. Something clicked when I looked at it. I set down the briefcase, walked to the bin, took hold of a corner of the paint-smudged stiff brown paper, and pulled it out. A handful of dust devils and bits of excelsior flew up into the air and settled down upon the freshly swept floor.

"Hey!" the janitor complained. "I'm tryin' to get this place cleaned up!"

I dug into my pocket and handed him a bill. That choked off the complaints. I unfolded the stiff, crumpled-up paper which I'd spotted as a stencil and stretched it out to its full length. It wasn't too difficult to make out that the punched-out, ink-stained gaps spelled out Lambert Warehouse and Storage Co., 28 Pendleton St., Alexandria, Va. This was the place where the crates had been taken, and it stood to reason that someone at 28 Pendleton St., Alexandria, Va., should be receptive to information about Karl Erikson, to say nothing of the contents of the briefcase.

I dropped the stencil back into the bin, wiped off my hands with a bit of excelsior, and left the office with the janitor's thanks following me down the hall. I stood on the Fifth Avenue curb trying to hail a cab, and I had the feeling I was on a treadmill. All roads might not lead to Rome, but in Karl Erikson's case they apparently led to the very near vicinity of Washington, D.C.

I had to wait forty minutes at La Guardia for the next commuter flight to Washington. I used most of it sitting in the snack bar, making up for a few of the meals I'd missed recently. This was after a trip to the men's room to get the rest of the stencil ink off my hands.

I picked up a copy of the *Daily Mirror* because that paper carries the more sensational crime stories and I'm always interested in reading about activity in my former line of work. Bank robberies had been in short supply the previous day, however, and I turned to the sports pages and checked out the action at Aqueduct and the other eastern tracks. I knew Hazel had a little something riding almost every day, but I didn't find the names of any of her favorites.

I was refolding the paper when an item in the general news caught my eye. The Justice Department had asked for a postponement in a case brought against alleged syndicate members "to allow time for the introduction of new evidence now in the process of preparation for presentation to this court." The defense had objected strenuously, but the trial judge had granted the delay.

The briefcase resting against my leg seemed to press a little harder. The odds against the briefcase material being the evidence mentioned in the newspaper article were the same as the odds against the first successful moon shot. But *somebody* in reasonably high-up government circles wanted the material in the briefcase, or Karl Erikson never would have been sent after it.

From the look of it, certainly, it was destined to be evidence in a courtroom somewhere if only I could place it in the right hands.

I boarded the plane and spent eighty minutes in fruitless speculation about ways to break through the barrier of official silence surrounding Erikson. With the usual undercover agencies' need-to-know restrictions there probably weren't too many men who could talk about Erikson knowledgeably even if they wanted to.

We arrived at National Airport just after another rain shower. Wisps of steam were drifting upward from the greasy, brown surface of the sluggish Potomac River as the approach pattern carried us across it. The newly present bright sunlight promised a hot, humid afternoon.

I followed the alighting passengers through the terminal until I located a bank of pay phones. I looked in the yellow pages of the phone directory for the Lambert Warehouse and Storage Company. A phone call might be able to tell me a good deal about Lambert.

I wasn't too surprised to learn that there was no Lambert Warehouse and Storage Company listed in the yellow pages or in the white pages either. With the shortcut eliminated I went out to the cab rank, wondering if I was wasting cab fare checking out a nonexistent address.

At least it was a fairly short ride. And there was a Pendleton Street, a narrow paved lane that sloped from the main section of Alexandria toward the river. Pendleton Street came to a dead end at Royal Street, which paralleled the Potomac. Layer upon layer of resurfacing had covered the street until only a few of the original eighteenth century cobblestones showed through. The present day curbstones were mere ridges.

There was even a 28 Pendleton Street. It was an old, four-story brick structure that might have been a brewery at one time. It was surrounded by abandoned shops and broken-glassed buildings in such profusion that it was obvious that time had not done well by this section of old Alexandria.

At first I couldn't see anything which identified the building. Then high on the front wall, off-center from the entrance, I saw a very small sign which said Lambert Warehouse and Storage Co. Both the size of the sign's lettering and its placement indicated that Lambert didn't believe in advertising itself. Since I was now sure there was a Lambert, I paid off the cab.

The concern hardly looked prosperous. Only the heavy, glass, double doors and the concrete steps leading up to them were new. But there were anachronisms in the building's outwardly dilapidated condition. I could see through the windows that the interior was illuminated by modern fluorescent light fixtures. And each window was bordered with electronic alarm tape. Further inspection showed closed-circuit television lenses projecting from the beaks of open-mouth gargoyles at the corners of the building. Lambert's was protected by a sophisticated security system that would furnish a challenge to the very best technicians.

The real giveaway, though, was the parking lot. There must have been three hundred cars parked there, and not a one of them looked more than three years old. Lambert's employees were evidently quite well-to-do, a prosperity synonymous with a government pay check in most areas adjacent to the nation's capitol.

I climbed the concrete steps and passed through the heavy glass doors. I expected to be intercepted at once, in view of the other precautions, but when I wasn't, I noticed electronic eyes imbedded in the burnished aluminum door frames which signaled my entrance to someone. Whether out in the open or on a closed-circuit television screen, someone inside Lambert's was monitoring my visit.

A long counter extended the width of the twenty-foot lobby, effectively blocking it except for a door at one end which had no handle but was opened by a key. Beyond the counter, under the fluorescent lights was a large open room crowded with long rows of desks. Most were occupied by attractive girls pounding typewriters or thumbing through tightly packed open-face files.

Lambert's might have been an old building, but the office equipment was new. Banks of metal file cabinets butted side by side ranged three walls of the huge room. A glance was enough to assure an observer that the cabinets could hold records for a great deal more storage than a building the size of Lambert's could accommodate. Whatever went on here extended far beyond the capacity of this single building. The office layout looked far more like the central accounting department of a large insurance company than a riverside warehouse.

No one paid the slightest attention to me as I stood at the counter. I propped the briefcase up on it in full view, and a head or two turned in my direction, but nothing happened. Two miniskirted girls at nearby desks huddled in earnest girl talk. They glanced at me once as if to guage my importance, then went back to their conversation.

I cleared my throat loudly. The nearest girl, a gum-chewing blonde, said something impatient to her friend. She disengaged herself from her desk and strolled to the counter. Her skirt must have just met establishment standards. Above it she was wearing a sleeveless knit pull-over whose twin highlights appeared to project a quarter of the way across the counter toward me. "Yes?" she inquired with a set smile which displayed irregular teeth, a demonstration of the law of life that no one has everything.

I pointed to the briefcase. "I'm turning this in for Mr. Erikson," I said, hoping the name would register. "Mr. Karl Erikson."

The blonde gave no sign that the name meant anything to her. She looked toward the rear of the room where a group of men were clustered around a soft drink vending machine. "Mr. Harrington is in charge of returns," she informed me. "He'll be with you in a moment."

She sauntered toward the vending machine with a hip sway that would have done credit to a contestant in the Miss America pageant. I saw her speak to one of the men, who glanced in my direction, nodded, then continued talking to his companions. Mr. Harrington was a sandy-haired, bespectacled young man, and it was for much longer than a moment that he continued his conversation.

I'd already made up my mind to dislike Mr. Harrington by the time he crumpled his paper cup and dropped it into a waste container. Even then he detoured en route to the counter to pass a desk where a languorous looking brunette was sitting at a card punch machine. He spent another two minutes with her, from their mutual smiles evidently relaying the dirty joke he had just picked up at the soft drink machine. Finally he deigned to walk to the counter. "Turn in?" he asked in a world-weary tone.

"That's right," I said, trying to keep my voice civil.

"Where's your form 357?"

"My what?"

Behind his spectacles Mr. Harrington's weak-looking eyes expressed boredom. He was bored with me, and he was bored with himself. "Your record of withdrawal and return. If you took it out, you signed for it."

"I didn't take it out. I'm just returning it."

"Oh, you want it placed in dead storage, is that it?"

"Correct. To be marked for Mr. Karl Erikson."

Harrington also gave no sign that the name meant anything to him. "You've got the proper release to authorize our acceptance?"

"Release?"

This time Harrington looked pitying. "Form 684B. Didn't your office give you one?"

I took a stab. "I was told you'd give me a receipt."

Harrington shook his head. "Someone's putting you on, friend. You must be new. I remember I went through the same routine when I started with the State Department. They had me chasing all over town looking for a map of China showing the location of Poon Tang." He tittered on a high-pitched note. A limp-wristed gesture of his long-fingered, narrow hands invited me to appreciate his situation. "How many places have you been steered to today trying to unload this briefcase?"

"You mean you won't take it?"

His supercilious half-smile faded. "Not without a form 684B, certainly. And not without the chain and handcuff attachment which goes with this type of courier case." For the first time he evinced curiosity. "Where did you say you got it?"

"From Karl Erikson."

"Well, then I suggest you take it back to this Mr. Erikson, whoever he is, and tell him I think he's carrying his little joke a bit too far." Mr. Harrington's thin lips screwed up in distaste. "With friends like this Erikson you don't need enemies. I think he's setting you up for a hard time." The foppish young man looked me over more carefully than he had previously. "If you're actually in unauthorized possession of classified material, you're going to have to do a lot of explaining to someone. You know I have to make out an incident report on this, don't you?"

"Incident report?" I sounded like a damned parrot.

"Any irregularity in procedure must be reported the same day," Mr. Harrington said solemnly. He didn't seem displeased about it.

I looked at the briefcase sitting on the counter, mocking me in my effort to get rid of it. Young Mr. Harrington's expression seemed no less mocking, although I might have exaggerated it. At any rate I wasn't doing any good with him, and I'd had enough of him. I leaned across the counter as though to speak confidentially. "There's one thing I'm curious about," I said.

"What's that?"

"Did you ever find Poon Tang?" Young Mr. Harrington stared at me uncomprehendingly. "And would you know what to do with it if you did?"

"Oh, you're one of those," he said haughtily and flounced away from the counter. He returned to a glass-partitioned office and immediately picked up his telephone. I grabbed the briefcase from the counter and headed for the door. I couldn't afford any question-and-answer sessions with any official types summoned by the perturbed Mr. Harrington's phone call. His remark about unauthorized possession of classified material had carried a hard core of truth.

"Damn all regulation-bound pretty boys, anyway," I muttered to myself as I ran down the concrete steps.

I set off along Pendleton Street toward the center of Alexandria in long strides.

It had been foolish to provoke the foppish Mr. Harrington. He had made clear two things of which I was previously unaware: (1) no government office of the Lambert Warehouse type would accept a pig in a poke, and (2) if anything went wrong in my attempt to get rid of the briefcase, I had no one to speak for me to account for my possession of it.

And right now I wasn't sure where to go except to put distance between myself and anything the fragile Harrington had set in motion.

SIX

I HAD to wait for a traffic signal at Washington Street. The macadam near the curb was bubbling slowly in the muggy heat. I hurried across the intersection as soon as the light turned green, already uncomfortably sticky.

Exactly what was I supposed to do now with the damn briefcase? I was tempted to leave it in a bus station or train station locker and mail the ticket to Lambert's, but that type of solution wasn't going to do Karl Erikson any good.

The thought of Erikson suggested another tack. If I couldn't backtrack to his organization via the briefcase, why not forget that route and seek information by the direct approach method? I couldn't lose any more ground than I had already.

I flagged down a Veterans' cab cruising north on Washington Street almost at the intersection of Patrick. "The Navy Department in the District," I told the cabbie. I sank back and tried to enjoy the breeze whipped up by our passage as our route took us over the Memorial Bridge to a three-story building on Constitution Avenue near the Lincoln Memorial.

I climbed the outside stairs and was met by a young sailor in whites with an SP brassard around his left arm and a .45 caliber service revolver holstered on his hip. "Yes, sir?" he inquired.

"I'm trying to locate a Navy man," I said. "At least he was once. You keep personnel records here, don't you?"

The sailor turned me over to a chief petty officer. "Officer, petty officer, or enlisted man?" the chief asked when I explained.

"Officer," I said. "Commander."

"Then you want room 240, the Officer Locator Center. Take this corridor—" he pointed "—to room 236 and turn right."

I found a door with a placard on it reading 240—Officer Locator. Inside there was the inevitable counter behind which battleship-gray metal desks were aligned in orderly ranks. A redhaired, freckle-faced WAVE with a scribe insignia on the sleeve of her blue tunic greeted me. "May I help you, sir?" she asked.

"I hope so. I've lost touch with a Commander Karl Erikson, a reserve officer. He's still in government in some capacity. Can you help me locate him or the office where he works?"

"We'll try, sir. Which branch of the Navy is he with?"

"I was hoping you could tell me that."

The WAVE pulled a ruled card from a cubbyhole containing cards of different colors and placed it in front of me, then offered me the use of a ballpoint pen anchored to the counter by a chain. "If you'll fill out this request for locator service card, sir, I'm almost sure we can help."

I glanced at the multilined, closely printed card with its various categorizations. I felt the barrier of red tape encircling me again. "I'm afraid I can't begin to supply the information requested by this card," I said. "That's why I'm here."

"Just fill out the spaces you can," the WAVE told me. "We've got all kinds of cross-reference data, so even a few facts would be helpful. His serial number especially."

"I don't know that." I tried to think of the little I knew about Erikson's background. I remembered him rigging the short wave radio in the bar at Key West before we went to Cuba. "He was in communications for a while. And he was in Vietnam early."

"Put it down," the WAVE advised. "Put down everything you can remember."

Most of the spaces on the card were still blank after I filled in the little I knew. The WAVE took the card from me and punch-dialed a number on the counter-top phone and read off the meager data to someone at the other end of the line. She spelled out the letters of the name Erikson phonetically.

She looked at me with the phone still in her hand. "They want to know if Commander Erikson is on active duty now?"

"I don't know, but I don't think so." There was almost no way he could have been on active duty, considering some of our escapades together. The Navy wouldn't have wanted its coattails that near the grease pit.

The WAVE spoke into the phone again, then hung up. I expected some computer with its limitless memory bank would search its magnetic brain and spit out the information instantly, but automation apparently hadn't progressed that far in the Navy. Seven or eight minutes elapsed before the counter-top phone went brrrttt in a muted ring.

The WAVE picked it up and listened. She started to say something, stopped, looked at me, and placed the phone on the counter. "Excuse me just a second, sir," she said. She walked to a desk in the rear of the room where a jg lieutenant was seated.

The WAVE spoke to him in a low tone. The lieutenant looked at me, shook his head negatively, then said something to the WAVE. She came back to the counter.

"Any problem?" I asked casually.

"Do you have security clearance, sir?"

"I'm afraid not."

She picked up the phone again. "No clearance," she

said into it. "Yes, I understand. No, of course not. Yes, sir."

She replaced the phone in its cradle and faced me again, her previously pleasant-looking freckled face wearing a closed look. "I'm sorry, sir, but I'm afraid we can't be of any help except to confirm there is a Commander Karl Erikson who is a member of the Naval Reserve. Any information concerning Commander Erikson is classified, though, and cannot be given out by this office. That's all I can tell you."

She glanced over her shoulder at the jg leiutenant who nodded approvingly. I hated to accept the brushoff, but I had a feeling from the way the lieutenant was watching me that if I appeared too inquisitive, he'd intervene with a few questions of his own.

"Thanks anyway," I said to the WAVE and left quickly. When I reached the sidewalk, I turned up Constitution Avenue toward the Ellipse. I found a bench on the Mall and sank down upon it while crowds of tourists streamed by. I looked at the briefcase at my feet. Once again I was tempted to say the hell with it and take off for the mountain valley surrounding Ely, Nevada. The WAVE's red hair had reminded me of Hazel's chestnut mane. No one had a gun in my back forcing me to continue this frustrating pilgrimage in Washington's ungodly heat.

I counted my money, putting aside enough for one-way fare to Reno. At the rate I'd been spending, my available cash could only last another day or two anyway. But to what point? What could I try that had any better chance of success? If only Jock McLaren had been in that phony export-import office in New York—

McLaren.

When Erikson and I had been inside the bank vault, he said something about having dinner with McLaren at his home in Arlington. I hoisted myself from the bench, conscious of how hot, sticky, and dirty I felt. I walked along the Mall until I found a phone booth.

The Arlington directory listed nine McLarens. I sifted through the change in my pocket. I had only three dimes. I left the booth long enough to stop groups of tourists and beg change for quarters, then stepped back inside the booth and stacked the dimes up on the shelf.

I planned to ask the same question of all phone answerers: "Is Jock at home?" I ran through six McLaren phone numbers who had never heard of Jock. On the seventh dime a pleasant feminine voice responded that Jock was at work at the Old Treasury Building Annex on Twenty-Second Street.

"Could you give me his office phone, please? Is this Mrs. McLaren? It's important."

The timbre of the feminine voice changed. "Call the Treasury Department," she said. "If your business is official, they'll give you his office phone number." She didn't sound as though she believed they would, though, when she hung up on me. I didn't even know if it was Mrs. McLaren; she had never identified herself. Erikson's wolf pack hid their trails well.

I glanced at my watch. Too late to call the Treasury now. The bureaucrats were in their smug Maryland and Virginia homes relaxing over cocktails. I'd call in the morning and see if I could get through to McLaren. Or should I take a chance and land on his doorstep tonight? I had his address on the directory page of McLarens I'd ripped from the phone book and put into my wallet.

I discarded the idea. Trying to bull my way past Jock's wife into his home could do me no good with McLaren. I'd try the Treasury Department in the morning.

But that meant another overnight stay. A few years before when in Washington I'd stayed at the Carroll Arms Hotel near Union Station. The setting sun had cooled things off somewhat. In a burst of frugality I began walking. At Fourteenth Street I turned left to Pennsylvania Avenue and then began the hike crosstown. There was the usual crowd waiting for the Virginia buses at Twelfth

Street, but otherwise, pedestrian traffic on the streets had already thinned out.

I stopped in a haberdashery and bought a white shirt. The one I was wearing was beginning to feel permanently attached to me. So was my underwear, but I could do something about that at the hotel.

The walk to the Carroll Arms was relaxing, and I arrived in a better mood than I'd been in all day. I checked in, had dinner, bought a cigar and a newspaper at the newsstand, and went up to the room. I stripped down and put underwear and socks to soak in the wash basin while I took a hot shower. I hand scrubbed my laundry afterward and hung everything over the shower-curtain bar.

Wrapped in a thin-threaded towel, I sat down in the room's armchair with cigar and newspaper. The world news on page one was depressing enough to make me turn the page. I scanned pages two and three, and was halfway through an item of local news before I realized it had personal implications. I sat up straighter and began it again.

The headline said "NO CLUES IN VETERAN'S DEATH." The story began:

Police today confirmed they had no suspects in the torture death of Vietnam veteran William Long, 32, whose badly beaten body was found yesterday in Rock Creek Park. Contents of a National Airlines carry-on flight bag were scattered around the body. Detective James Nolan stated that Long's landlady said he had just returned yesterday morning from a ten day vacation in Nassau. Long, who had been badly wounded in Vietnam, sustaining facial burns requiring extensive plastic surgery, was still an outpatient at the Walter Reed Medical Center. Police today were checking Long's friends and acquaintances for possible clues.

I dropped the paper on the floor and studied the ash on the tip of my cigar. A man who had received extensive plastic surgery had returned from Nassau yesterday, the same day I had, and had been tortured and killed. Had the long arm of the syndicate reached out, thinking it was my plastic surgery?

But why Washington? How had they known to look in Washington? I hadn't said anything to Candy or Chen Yi about Washington. But then a memory intruded. During the dimly recalled, brandy-dazed hours in the Incense Room, hadn't I offhandedly said "Washington" when the blond Hermione inquired where I was from?

Candy Kane had said forthrightly that Hermione was a gangster's girl. With the hullabaloo in underworld Nassau about the rifling of the syndicate's safe deposit boxes, she could have mentioned to her boy friend the stranger she'd met. She could have described me. In fullest detail actually, considering the nude circumstances of our romp together.

Considering circumstances of my escape from syndicate goons at the Oakes Field airstrip, any hint at all would have been seized upon eagerly by syndicate henchmen. And that poor devil Long had had the bad luck to return with his scarred face from Nassau the very day they were looking for me.

Whoever grabbed him would have to be stupid not to know before too long that they had the wrong man, but Long's really bad luck was that this crowd left no witnesses. They killed him, and now they were still looking for me. I had no way to hide a face easily remembered by anyone who had been in my company as long as Hermione had been. At Hazel's ranch I had hair pieces and makeup which could change my appearance considerably but none of it was here.

It was my good fortune that someone had discovered Long's body and an alert reporter had covered the story so that it appeared in tonight's paper. Otherwise I might have walked right into someone's arms when I was ready to leave town. Airline terminals were surely being checked for scar-faced men with any kind of luggage that might contain what the mobsters wanted to retrieve.

I looked at the briefcase sitting on the floor at the foot of the bed. That innocent-looking item was double dynamite now. If I couldn't get any satisfaction at the Treasury Department in the morning, the briefcase and I were going to get out of Washington fast. But not together. Oh no, not together.

I went to bed, but my sleep was fitful. I was downstairs in the morning before the coffee shop opened. I bought a paper to see if there were any further developments in the Long case, but the morning *Post*'s item was almost identical with the story carried in the previous evening's *Star*.

I went back to the room after coffee and Danish to wait impatiently until I figured government offices would be open. I'd already verified from the torn-out phone directory page that McLaren's first name was Albert. I'd always known him only as Jock. I dialed the Treasury Department number, waited for three rings, and then heard a bright-voiced "Treasury Department; good morning."

"Good morning," I replied. "I'd like to speak to Albert McLaren. He's a Treasury Department employee, but I don't know in what section."

"Let me check our alphabetical index, sir." There was a silence broken only by the sound of rustling pages. "I'm sorry, sir," the operator's voice said finally. "Mr. McLaren is in a section which can only be reached through a classified extension number. Do you know the extension?"

"No, I don't."

"Then I'm afraid you'll have to contact Mr. McLaren outside business hours, sir."

There was a click, and the connection was gone.

So that was that.

I didn't have to think what to do because I'd already planned it. I checked out of the Carroll Arms and walked down the hill to Union Station. In the concourse I found a shop that sold luggage. I bought a fiberboard case of the type college students used to send dirty laundry home to mother before the country became so affluent. Then I placed the briefcase in the laundry box. I used crumped pages from my *Washington Post* to serve as padding. When I finally buckled the cloth straps around the laundry box, the briefcase was secure.

Washington's main post office is just down the street from Union Station. I carried the laundry box there and filled out a label that fit into the metal frame riveted to the cover. I addressed the label to Hazel Andrews, Rancho Dolorosa, Ely, Nevada. I made out the return address the same way. Then I stepped up to the air parcel post window and paid $7.35 to mail the case.

Back in Union Station I purchased a Senator Claghorn, Virginia plantation hat and pulled it down firmly around my ears. Hair piece wearers are told not to wear hats, but this was an exception. I took a cab to National Airport, which seemed well on its way to becoming my semipermanent residence in this merry-go-round I found myself on.

I couldn't get to Salt Lake City in time to catch the once-a-day United flight to Ely which would have put me on the ground there shortly after noon.

I settled for the 10:30 A.M. United flight to Reno via Chicago. Then I called Hazel when I had myself ticketed. "I'm getting into Reno on the 3:35 P.M. flight from Washington, Big Stuff," I said to her. "How about picking me up?"

"Sure thing, Horseman," she responded cheerfully. "How did it go?"

"I'll tell you when I see you."

"That doesn't sound as though it went very well." Her voice was concerned.

"I'll tell you when I see you," I repeated and hung up.

Nobody bothered me or—so far as I could tell—even noticed me when I boarded the Reno plane.

I slept better on the westbound flight than I had the previous night. It's a 320 mile drive between Ely and

Reno, and even the way Hazel drives, it takes seven hours. I had time for a meal before she showed up at the airport. She had on her usual ranch costume of sleeveless buckskin vest, levis, and silver-conched cowboy boots. "Hi, lover," she said and kissed me.

I waited till we were in the parking lot in her Corvette before I told her what had happened. She listened intently, her capable hands gripping the motionless steering wheel. "You mean Erikson is stuck there?" she interrupted me at one point. "Won't his agency brass hats get him out?"

"I believe they will in time," I answered. "But right now I'm the only one who knows where he is, and I can't break through to let anyone know."

"It's the craziest thing I ever heard." Hazel started up the Corvette and eased out of the parking lot into traffic.

I told her about the syndicate involvement and the possibility they knew where to look for Erikson. And about the laundry case I'd mailed to the ranch. The only thing I didn't tell her was the tragedy of the scar-faced veteran in Washington. I didn't want her upset about the syndicate's fast reaction time.

Hazel rocketed the Corvette along Highway 80 east and turned off on Alternate 95 to Fallon. She hadn't eaten, so we stopped for a sandwich at the casino in the center of town. Back on the road she really used that automobile. Every time I glanced across the front seat at her profile her flaming red hair was standing straight out in the breeze of our ninety-mph passage along Route 50.

At one point she passed a truck on a hill. I unclenched my hands forcibly after we got back into our own lane at a point that seemed like ten yards from the top. "Do you think Karl Erikson is in physical danger?" Hazel asked, breaking a silence that had lasted for fifty miles and seemingly not at all concerned that a lot of hardworking horsepower could have been coming from the other direction and challenged us severely.

I found I'd been avoiding her question in my own mind.

Hazel removed her eyes from the road to look at me. "Watch what the hell you're doing, woman!" I growled, but I was aware that my irritation was more with myself than with her.

Another mile of highway buzzed past us in a blur of telephone poles that looked like a picket fence. "Not really," I finally said in answer to her question. "Not in Nassau with British-style justice involved . . ."

My voice trailed off. What did I know about British-style justice? Candy Kane had already indicated to me some of the crackerbox aspects of Bahamian security. And were Bahamian officials any more immune to the payoff than their US counterparts?

The conversation lapsed again. We stopped for gas in Austin, and Hazel switched on the headlights when we started up the curving ascent leading through the first of the seven-thousand-foot passes between us and Ely. Night driving in Nevada makes me nervous. Cattle graze freely along the roadsides, and every so often one ambles into a car. Hazel drove with the blithe unconcern of a native.

It was 9:30 when we passed through Eureka with another seventy-five miles to go. We made it in a whole lot less than seventy-five minutes, Hazel slowing down just slightly on the five-mile stretch between Ruth and Ely with the Kennecott Copper Company's open-pit mines off to the right.

She pulled into Ashworth's Chevron Station in the center of Ely. "I want to talk to Bud about the pickup," she explained.

"Okay," I said, easing out of the Corvette. "I'm going to wet my whistle at Greg's."

Greg's Club was a few doors up the street. I planked my butt on a bar stool and ordered Jim Beam on the rocks. Greg's was one of the few places in town that didn't have even a slot machine on the premises. Greg sold booze, period. He'd been selling it at the same location since 1929, having antedated Repeal by a bit. He told me once he used to sell wine from hogsheads stacked along one wall and even in that sparsely settled area he sold eight thousand gallons. When the sun beats down on Nevada valleys with nothing growing more than waist high, people develop a thirst.

Hazel came in and sat down beside me, and I ordered a grasshopper for her. "I forgot to tell you I took delivery on the plane while you were away," she said. "I still say you shouldn't have done it."

"That's me, kid," I said. "Not even a box of chocolates in three years, then an airplane."

Hazel had been taking flying lessons. I'd come back from New York after my last job with Erikson with a bundle of cash he hadn't known about, and without saying anything to Hazel I'd ordered ninety-six-thousand-dollar's worth of airplane for her, a Cessna 301 with special navigational equipment. It was a twin-engine job. Single engines make me as nervous as night driving on Nevada highways.

"You'll have to speed up your flying lessons now, to say nothing of getting checked out in the Cessna," I said. "How long will it take?"

"A month if there's good flying weather every day."

"Did you pay for it?"

"Yes," she confirmed. "Your bankroll didn't stretch quite that far, so I pitched in the last chunk."

She was qualified to do it. Her ranch might not have been too much by Texas standards, but it was a fair piece of property. Most of it was given over to grazing land for beef cattle. After the death of her mother Hazel had been left the original small homestead acreage, her birthplace, by her stepfather.

She'd added to it from funds acquired as the widow of Blue Shirt Charlie Andrews, the gambler who bet 'em higher than a duck could fly, and her second husband, a saturnine man of mystery who left her the Dixie Pig, a tavern on the west coast of Florida where I'd first met her, plus stocks, bonds, and cash till she needed a money manager to keep track of things.

In other words Hazel wasn't hurting and wasn't about to be. When we'd first hit it off together, it had taken me a while to break her of the playful habit of leaving hundred dollar bills under my plate for walking-around money. She hated to see me broke because she was afraid I'd go back to my former pastime of robbing banks, which for years had been both vocation and avocation with me. She liked to have me with her at the ranch.

But that had been before Karl Erikson muscled his way into my life. Hazel liked Erikson and had even abetted his recruitment of me. She had managed at times to include herself in Erikson-generated situations. Her roles were intended to be peripheral, but at least once it had turned out to be a good deal more than that. I knew I was going to hear more from Hazel about Karl Erikson's present predicament.

"Another drink?" I asked her.

She declined. We said good night to Greg and went back to the car. Hazel headed north toward her ranch situated in the higher country between Ely and McGill, the copper-smelting town that processed Kennecott's ore.

We turned in from the highway on the dirt road, which was straight as a string for a mile and a half until we left the valley for the hills. I got out and opened the gate when we reached the fenced-in portion, closing and looping it shut again after Hazel drove the Corvette inside.

The headlights wandered along the curving road to the ranchhouse. To pick me up in Reno, Hazel had been on the road for fifteen hours, another reason I had bought her the plane. Except that the aircraft manufacturer now had my cash for a plane she was probably two months away from flying, and my bankroll consisted of what was in my pocket, not a stimulating amount.

"Let's move it upstairs, Earl," Hazel said when we were in the kitchen. I knew she'd had a hard day, and I was ready for bed myself. I followed her upstairs. She was standing in the middle of the floor in our bedroom when I entered. Her boots were already off, and her vest, levis, and underwear floated onto a chair. She came over to me and put her arms around my waist.

"I thought you'd be too tired," I said.

"I'm never too tired for that, Horseman," she said in her deep voice. "Horseman" is her pet name for me. We both go way back in wagering on the comparative speed of thoroughbred horses.

She assisted with my undressing. The feel of her hun-dred-and-fifty-pound, naked female body in such close proximity to mine sent exciting messages to my nerve ends. I love big women, and Hazel is big everywhere it counts, besides being in better shape than the average pro football player.

We sat down upon the edge of the bed. Four hands played a brisk duet upon two bodies. Hazel pulled me over backward on the bed, and we wrestled exuberantly, each striving to be uppermost. I pinned her finally and climbed aboard the solid platform of her firm belly.

"Make it a good one!" she murmured huskily, widen-ing to receive me.

I wrung myself out in the effort to make it a good one. Hazel's shrill yips in my ear testified that I was doing something right. Some nights it's not possible to ford a dry creekbed, and then at other times everything is a wide, free-flowing river. We had antepenultimate, penultimate, and final soft explosions.

Afterward Hazel extracted two cigarettes from a pack on the night table, lit them, and handed me one. We were side by side on the bed on our backs. "When are we going to Nassau to get Erikson out of that jail?" she said to me.

"When are we WHAT?" I said it so vehemently I blew a shower of sparks from my cigarette. We both batted at them furiously to keep the bed from catching fire. "What the hell did you say?"

"You know you can't leave him there," Hazel said calmly. "If you can't get anyone in Washington to act, that leaves you."

"The hell it does. I played it by the book. I lugged that damn briefcase all over Washington trying to put it into the right hands and my story into the right ears. I told you what happened."

But Hazel has a one-track mind. In all respects. "If no one in Washington is going to help, what would it take to free him?"

"Why do you keep harping on this?" I demanded.

"Because I know you, Horseman. In a few days you'll be sneaking up behind me and mumbling, 'Look, dear, there's this little bit of unfinished business in Nassau, and —well—see you later.'" Hazel bounded from her back to her knees and glared down at me. "And I won't have you running out on me. We're going together."

"I'm not going anywhere, baby. I've been the route on that damned island, and there's no future in it. Although if I could just think of something that promised to have a chance of—"

"See?" she exclaimed triumphantly. "What did I tell you?"

"Forget it," I said.

"What would it take to get him out? Really?"

"If Candy was leveling with me, not too much to spring him from the jail. But getting off New Providence would be another sack of spuds. Even a spook plane would have a hard time getting in and out of there again after the commotion I caused when I blew the scene."

"You'd think the government would do something for him after all he's done for them," Hazel said in a resentful tone.

"Everyone in the damn government is in a conspiracy to keep me from letting the right people know. That's the problem."

"What about this man McLaren in New York?"

"I told you I've already tried that. His wife wouldn't give me any information and neither would the Treasury Department."

"Suppose I called Mrs. McLaren right now and said I was from Commander Erikson's office?"

I hesitated. "I don't think it would work."

"Do you still have the McLaren phone number?"

"The part of the page I tore from the phone directory is still in my wallet." Hazel slithered from the bed and padded to my pants on the floor. "Have you forgotten it's well after midnight there?"

"All the better. It will sound like a real emergency." She was going through my wallet. "What happened to your money?"

"I buried it at the foot of the Statue of Liberty. Don't be so damned nosy."

Hazel sniffed. She came back to the bed, large as life and twice as nude, and picked up the phone. "Person-to-person to Mrs. Albert McLaren in Arlington, Virginia," she said and gave the number.

There was a long silence. "It won't work," I said. "There must be some sort of code call-in used. There'd have to be."

"That's why hitting her fast this time of night before she gets her brain in gear might pay off," Hazel said coolly. "If—" She stopped speaking. From where I was on the bed I could hear the sleepy-sounding "Hello?" from the receiver. I scrambled up and shoved in alongside Hazel who canted the receiver so I could hear, too.

"Sorry to bother you this time of night, Mrs. McLaren," Hazel's rich, confident-sounding contralto rolled across the miles. "I'm calling from Commander Erikson's office, and it's urgent that we speak to your husband immediately."

"Oh, I'm so sorry," Mrs. McLaren said. "Jock left for Miami this morning, and I know he's going on beyond that, but I don't know where."

Hazel looked at me. "Hang up," I whispered.

"Thanks very much, Mrs. McLaren," she said smoothly. "We'll follow through on that." She hung up. "Well?" she said to me.

"I'll bet McLaren is going on to Nassau. I can think of a sequence that might have brought it about, too. If he came back into the New York office after I was there and the office manager type told him about the joker trying to unload a briefcase for Erikson and described me, McLaren might have checked back with his people and found out that Erikson was overdue and unreported. Then he might have been sent to Nassau to monitor the situation and see what was needed to be done. In which case anything we tried to do would just be interference or plain spinning our wheels."

"You're not really buying that selling job you just did on yourself, are you?" Hazel asked scornfully.

I fixed her with my beadiest eye. "Woman, if you think well of the twenty-one-carat, mint condition of your prodigiously bare ass, don't bug me. I'm going to sleep."

And I did.

SEVEN

In the cold light of morning, of course, I found myself going all over it again in my mind. I slipped out of bed without waking Hazel, then went down to the kitchen and heated up the coffee that remained in the percolater. I carried a steaming cup to the kitchen window, and not even the battery-acid taste of the coffee could detract from a sky so incredibly blue as to be unbelievable anywhere else except in the high country.

My thoughts kept running in the same worn channel: there must be *something* I could do to break through the official barrier of government silence surrounding Karl Erikson. The real problem was that a lot of avenues open to the average individual were closed to me. I couldn't call the nearest FBI office and tell them to come and get an item vital to the national security. With my background, when they got through asking questions about how I'd acquired it plus a few assorted queries about my past, it wouldn't take a judge and jury long to decide that I owed Uncle a lot of time. And they'd be right, not that I had any intention of queuing up to pay that piper.

It was such a beautiful morning that I decided to do something I'd had in the back of my mind for some time, ever since the wasted trip to New York, and that was to sight in the Smith & Wesson .38 police special I'd lifted from Erikson's old office. On the ranch property a mile away there was a gravel pit used to repair the ravages of wind erosion, rain, and snow on the ranch road, and it made an excellent backstop I'd used before.

I left the ranch house via the kitchen door and went down the path to the barn, a low, sprawling, added-onto structure behind which were the head-high, split-rail corrals used at branding time. I started up the Jeep and let it idle, then walked to a corner of the barn where an open trailer was loaded with old tires. I ripped up a few cardboard cartons, rounded off the rough sections, and stuffed them into the tire centers to serve as targets.

I backed the Jeep to the trailer and hitched up to the load of tires. The last thing I did before taking off along the pine-bordered road to the gravel pit was toss three boxes of ammunition into the front seat of the Jeep.

I drove around the pit to its unscalped side, the side farthest removed from the ranch house. The hillside would serve as a sound baffle. Hazel never likes to hear my target practice. She always construes it as an indication I'll be leaving the ranch again shortly.

I stopped the jeep at the foot of the hillside and took a tire from the trailer and set it up on a high bank. I drew a rough circle in the center of the cardboard disk serving as a target, then backed off across the road. Balance and feel is everything in a hand gun, and this one felt right. I sighted in carefully on the circled target, using the right-hand-crossed-over-the-bracing-left-wrist method, and squeezed off five shots.

The grouping was high and slightly to the right when I crossed the road and examined the target. I turned the tire around and went back across the road. The second grouping followed the same pattern. So this .38 shot slightly high and to the right. Later I'd do something about its sight, but for now it was enough to know it and adjust for it.

Shooting a hand gun well is not something everyone can do. A lot of people can target shoot as I'd just done, sight-ing in the .38, but that's not real shooting. Wing shooting is the payoff. I'd learned this years before in an Oregon logging camp where I was avoiding the attention of a couple of irate police departments. I practiced in the woods every day for eighteen months, and when I came back to civilization, I could do things with a .38 that equaled the best I'd ever seen as a kid in the traveling Wild West shows.

Accessories are important to the hand-gun user. I've had people who are supposed to know tell me they'd never consider using a shoulder holster, which they call the slowest and most awkward place from which to get at a gun in a hurry. But a man has to go with what he knows, and I knew and reacted to my own shoulder holster as if it were a part of my flesh. The fact I was still walking around was fair testimony that a shoulder holster couldn't be all bad. I'd never been seriously tempted to find an alternative.

I tossed the target tire aboard the trailer, climbed back into the Jeep, and inched my way in four-wheel drive up a hillside trail slashed out of scrub oak and juniper with my ax and perspiration. At the top I pulled over to one side where I'd constructed a long, wooden, inclined chute which tilted downward over the rocky, brush-filled terrain. I loaded the tires aboard the trailer into the chute one behind the other. Way down below was a dangling rope which operated a bar gate in the chute and permitted me to release one tire at a time to go bounding down the craggy hillside.

I drove to the bottom of the hill and parked, then walked to the release rope, hefting the .38 balanced in my palm. When I pulled on the rope, a tire rolled from the chute and started down the hillside. It ran low through the brush with only an occasional little bounce into the air until it hit a rock and jumped in a twenty-foot arc. It landed and swerved off at an angle only to hit another rock and zoom skyward again.

I had set self-imposed limits to a shooting area for these

free-running targets, and when they reached it, I never knew whether the tires would be high, low, left, right, or coming right at me. The idea was to let go three shots at each tire-target and score with two. This was wing shooting, and I'd learned it from an old hunter in Saskatchewan, but he was using a deer rifle and my effective range was only a fraction of his.

For twenty minutes I pulled the rope, released tires, and popped targets. When the chute was empty, I scoured the wooded area at the foot of the hill for the downed tires. I loaded them back onto the trailer. A gratifying number of the cardboard centers contained bullet punctures, some clean from wide-angle shots and others with long, ragged tears from almost head-on snap-shots.

But slogging through the brush, searching for tires, swatting at gnats, I was aware that my subconscious was still at work on the problem of Karl Erikson. I drove back up the hillside in a somber mood and reloaded the chute. When I returned to the house, I was planning to get out another hairpiece and do some experimenting with my makeup kit until I didn't resemble a war-scarred Vietnam veteran. Not that the syndicate could trace me to the ranch anyway.

I paused with the last tire in my hands, ready to insert it into the chute. The syndicate couldn't trace me to the ranch? Hermione had seen my scars and described them to her boy friend. Her description had been detailed enough so that the syndicate had tortured and killed Vietnam veteran William Long who must, in fact, have resembled me. And if Hermione had overheard Candy or Chen Yi mention my partner in a Nassau jail, she had undoubtedly reported that, too.

If the syndicate could get at Erikson in his jail cell or somehow remove him from it, the whole damned equation was changed.

Nobody stands up under torture forever. If the syndicate

got their hands on Erikson, my connection with the ranch wouldn't remain a secret from the syndicate forever. Which meant that if the syndicate got the chance to bear down on Erikson, I had not only led them to the ranch, I had led them to Hazel.

It didn't seem a critical possibility. Or at least standing on a Nevada hillside in the bright, clean, morning sunlight, I didn't think it seemed a critical possibility. Time was the essential item. It would take time for the syndicate to get at Erikson, assuming they didn't have someone already bought and paid for in the Nassau detention setup.

Erikson would assume that I had delivered the papers and they were safely in channels. He wouldn't deliberately turn the dogs on me, but in syndicate hands it was only a matter of time before his partner's name and likely hiding place became syndicate property. When a man cracks under torture, he tells what he knows and makes up what he thinks his torturers want to hear.

Time . . .

All of a sudden my options were reduced to one. I merely had to get Karl Erikson out of that Nassau jug before the syndicate did.

I dropped the tire still in my hands to the ground, left the loaded chute as it was, and drove down the hill again. Hazel was in the kitchen at the ranchhouse. "Ham and eggs?" she greeted me.

"Okay," I agreed. She moved toward the stove. "How'd you like to take a trip to Nassau?"

She turned, her expression the wide, beaming Hazel smile that makes the sun look like it's under a cloud. "Before or after breakfast?"

"After. How soon can you get someone in to look after things here?"

"I can call Jim Dodman. He's a retired career Army man and the handiest person I know looking after things and fixing things. I'm sure he could be here this afternoon."

"Call him."

Hazel started for the telephone in the front room, then stopped. "Why did you change your mind?"

"You converted me."

She snorted. "A likely story. Do you think Erikson is in danger?"

Hazel has a native shrewdness that is disconcertingly on target at times. "I think he wants to get out of there. Go make your phone call. What time does the mail get here?"

"The mail truck usually drops it off at the box out on the highway around noon. Why? Oh. The laundry case." She was silent for a moment. "What will you do with the material in it?"

"Get rid of it."

She started to ask another question, then changed her mind. She went into the front room, and I could hear her speaking on the phone. "He'll be here right after lunch," she reported upon her return to the kitchen.

I sat down at the table and watched her prepare a meal. We both worked our way through gorilla-sized portions of ham, eggs, toast, and coffee. "I'll be out in the barn," I told Hazel after my second cup of coffee.

She nodded. "I'll drive out to the highway for the mail as soon as I think it's here," she said.

I knew what I was going to do with the material in the briefcase. In the barn I rummaged through the stock of new and scrap lumber that had been accumulated by Hazel's deceased stepfather. The old man had been a crackerjack carpenter, which I was a long way from being, but I felt sure I could put together a box that would look like the crates I'd seen in the corridor of the Fifth Avenue office in New York.

I took saw and hammer down from the pegboard array of tools on one wall and set to work. Hazel's stepfather would have been horrified by the amount of lumber I wasted by measuring incorrectly twice, but I finally got the job done.

I searched around in the catchall drawers of the workbench until I found a half-empty can of encrusted black paint. I skimmed the crud from the surface, added some thinner, stirred the concoction with a stick, found a two-fingers-wide brush, and began lettering the crate. I didn't have a stencil, but had no difficulty in printing clearly.

I also had no difficulty in remembering the address. I lettered one side of the crate Lambert Warehouse and Storage Company, 28 Pendleton Street, Alexandria, Virginia. In smaller letters in one corner I put GSA—for Government Services Administration—1234510. Then I repeated the performance on the crate's other side. I wrote the fake order number down on a slip of paper and put the paper carefully into my wallet so I could use it to identify the crate when the time came.

When the crate was delivered to Lambert's with the fake order number, I figured that governmental obstinacy would ensure that it be set aside and held until the presumably missing waybill showed up. And held and held and held. Not until hell froze over, perhaps, but surely until I could interest someone in government in taking a look at a crate bearing GSA 1234510.

Hazel had come out to the barn to get the Jeep while I was still lettering. She returned with the mail, including the laundry case, while I was still admiring my handiwork. I took the case from Hazel, paused only to destroy the label with the local address, placed it in the crate without bothering to remove the briefcase from it, put the top of the crate on, and screwed it down with three-quarter-inch wood screws. "There," I said with satisfaction. "That thing's never going to come open by accident."

"Who's the Lambert Warehouse and Storage Company?" Hazel wanted to know.

"One of Erikson's blind pigs. The equivalent of a dead letter office for spook supplies in transit from one area to another. Or part of it is. The damned place is so big I don't really know what all they do there. Erikson probably—"

A bell began ringing loudly. "That's the house phone," Hazel said. "I don't know why I've always been too cheap to have an extension put out here." She sprinted up the path to the house with all her moving parts jiggling pleasantly.

She was back in three minutes. I was bending over the crate again, making sure the paint had soaked into the wood and was dry. It had and it was.

"Earl," Hazel said.

I spun around at the tension in her voice. "What is it?"

"Bud just called from Ashworth's Chevron station in town. Two men in a rented Chevrolet were just there asking directions to the Rancho Dolorosa. They wouldn't state their business, although Bud said he hinted around. He thought I'd want to know."

"He thought right," I said emphatically. "Put the man on your Christmas list."

"Who are the men, Earl?"

"I haven't the foggiest." Syndicate henchmen, who else? Although how had they gotten to Erikson this quickly? "But we're not waiting around to find out. D'you have any cash in the house?"

"Yes."

It had been a rhetorical question anyway. Hazel always had cash in the house and not just change in a teacup, either. Every once in a while we'd pack up on the spur of the moment and fly down to Tijuana and take a belt at the Caliente racetrack's 5-10. "Bring all of it. Don't pack anything, not even a toothbrush. We'll outfit in Miami. Move it!"

Hazel headed for the ranchhouse again while I picked up the crate and loaded it into the back of the Corvette. Then I changed my mind and transferred it to the Jeep. Those two types at the service station might have inquired what kind of car Hazel drove, and what the people in town usually saw was the Corvette.

I followed Hazel to the house, went upstairs and changed

clothes, swapped my brown hairpiece for a red one, and performed a quick facial changeover from the tubes in my makeup kit, which resembled a woman's small traveling case. I carried the kit downstairs. Hazel was in the kitchen. She had changed to a dress but was carrying only a large handbag. "I don't like it nearly as well when you give yourself that semiprettyboy appearance," she said disapprovingly when she looked me over.

"You know I've got to gild the lily a bit, or they wouldn't let me into the same hotel room with a gorgeous thing like you," I said.

She glanced at her watch. "We've missed the flight to Reno."

"Even if we hadn't, we wouldn't go near that airport," I said. "Our visitors might know who they're looking for."

"Then we're—"

"We're driving to Salt Lake City and flying to Miami from there," I interrupted her. "Let's go."

Outside I steered her to the Jeep. She raised an eyebrow but didn't say anything. I wanted to get out of there. The one thing I didn't want was to get pinned inside the ranch property by the two strangers reaching the gate before we did.

I breathed more freely when we cleared the gate. I knew the visitors weren't going to do themselves any good lining themselves up at the end of my .38, but I had Hazel to think about now, too.

"The connections may not be as good in Salt Lake City," Hazel objected when we reached the highway and I turned north.

"There's no sweat as long as we're leading this parade," I answered. I could have added that I was also instinctively following a life pattern that was a relic of my life-on-the-run days: never backtrack. You know there's trouble in that direction. You just don't know for sure what kind.

We made only one stop on the way to Salt Lake City. Hazel went off to powder her nose when I pulled up at a truck terminal in Wendover, Utah. The girl in the trucking office glanced casually at the printed address on the crate I'd carried inside and said it might be ten days before they had a full load going east. I said that was perfectly all right. I'd selected Wendover as the shipping point for the crate because it's just a few miles away from the Bonneville Salt Flats where the automotive speed records are broken. The local truckers are used to handling all kinds of freight.

I took my copy of the bill of lading and walked half a block to the Wendover post office. I purchased a stamped envelope, addressed it to Hazel at the ranch, marked the face of the envelope Hold at Post Office Box, stuffed the waybill into it, and dropped the envelope into the mail chute. The bill of lading would be at the Ely post office when I needed it. It was safer doing it that way than letting it go on to the ranch in case someone took an interest in the mail.

Hazel gave me an I-told-you-so look at the Salt Lake City airport when I learned that we had a choice of a five-hour layover or a trip to Miami via the Great Circle route. Well, almost. She brightened up, though, when I opted for the layover.

"With this kind of time on our hands the right kind of man would book us into the airport motel," she suggested. "So a girl could manage a little mattress testing."

We checked into the motel at the half-day rate, and Hazel took charge. We gave the mattress a brisk workout, showered, and then indulged in an unplanned nap which resulted in us dressing like firemen and running through the terminal to catch our flight.

Hazel slept again en route to Miami, but I didn't. As a man who has never been positive that Wilbur Wright had the absolutely one-hundred-percent correct idea, I like to have long periods on the ground between flights. Hazel's flight instructor at the Ely airport laughed when I confessed this to him. He said I'd get over it. Maybe, but it was one reason I'd gone for a chunk of extra cash to make Hazel's plane a twin-engine unit. Single-engine planes in the mountains of eastern Nevada gave me a lump in the throat that wouldn't go up or down.

A thought that had been pebble sized when it first occurred to me at the ranch had grown to boulder-size now that I'd had time for additional consideration. If the syndicate had traced me to the ranch, they must have obtained the information from Karl Erikson. But if that were true, how could he still be in a Nassau detention cell? And if he wasn't still in custody, what was I doing planning to go back there?

There was a way to find out.

I got rid of Hazel at Miami International Airport with the usual excuse. I found a phone booth near the men's room and removed from my wallet the cheaply printed card the bellman Roy had given me with Candy Kane's phone number on it. I called the number, hoping that Candy wouldn't answer the phone. I wouldn't get any useful information from him, but I might from the statuesque Chinese girl, Chen Yi.

"I'm sorry, sir," the operator's voice cut in after an interval, "but your party does not answer."

"Keep ringing, operator," I said. "There should be someone there."

There was a click at the other end of the line finally and a faint "Hello." It wasn't Candy's voice, and that had been my immediate concern. The voice was so low, though, that I thought I had a bad connection.

"Can you improve the connection, operator?" I asked.

"I can hear you," the voice at the other end of the line said more clearly, and I recognized Chen Yi's quiet manner of speaking.

"This is someone you met recently," I began.

"I recall the voice," she answered.

"Is Candy there? Can you speak freely?"

"He is not here."

"Can you tell me if the man in whom I was interested is still at the same location?"

"I do not know."

The Chinese girl's voice was lifeless with none of its usual vitality. "Has anything happened?" I asked.

"There has been a—an incident."

"An incident? What kind?"

"I do not wish to speak of it on the telephone."

I didn't like what I was thinking. "Listen, can I come and see you?"

"I do not advise it. Goodbye."

There was the click of a broken connection. I sat there staring at the phone in my hand before I hung up. I left the booth and went and collected Hazel. "We'll check into the airport motel here, too," I told her. "Then you grab a cab into town and get yourself outfitted at Burdine's. You know—touristy. Get me a jacket, a couple pairs of slacks, and three or four sportshirts. Make one outfit black. Plus underwear and socks." She knew my sizes. "And luggage to carry it in. Bring everything back to the motel."

"Why aren't you coming with me?"

"I'm going crosstown to pick up a couple of forgeries we'll need to get through customs in Nassau."

She held out her handbag, and I helped myself from the thick wad of bills in it. We caught separate cabs after I registered us into the motel. I directed the cab driver to a back street address, a print shop. In half an hour I had suitably inscribed, suitably aged, phony birth certificates that identified me as Rufus Barton and Hazel as Ernestine McClanahan Barton.

Miami was sticky hot. I saw an illuminated temperature indicator on a bank that said ninety-two degrees as another cab took me back to the airport. The humidity must have been close to 80 percent. I stopped at the Eastern flight desk in the terminal and booked two seats on the 9:00 P.M. to Nassau. In the motel room I stripped to my shorts and stretched out on the bed.

Hazel arrived two hours later. She came in laden with parcels, and that was only the beginning. The motel porter made two trips to deliver the boxes resulting from her shopping. Then he made still another trip to bring the new, empty suitcases. Hazel had a grand time displaying and modeling her purchases for herself before packing everything. She locked the suitcases and handed me the keys. "What time are we leaving?" she asked.

"Nine o'clock. I want to get there after dark."

A tiny frown creased her smooth forehead. "You're not expecting a welcoming committee?"

"I know I've changed my appearance, but I'd just as soon not have anyone looking at me in the daylight."

She didn't pursue it. We rested, had dinner at the airport, and read magazines until it was time for our flight. I couldn't concentrate on my reading. The short flight to Nassau was uneventful. After we stepped from the plane and went through the perfunctory identification and customs check with our forged documents, I steered Hazel toward the Paradise Island Hotel bus.

If I had to be away from the hotel for extended periods, and at the moment I had no idea, Hazel could amuse herself at the casino. Hazel has been known to derive quite a bit of amusement from a roulette wheel. The desk clerk at the hotel eyed me up and down when I admitted to having no reservations. "You're fortunate that this isn't the December-April interval, sir," he informed me loftily. I barely remembered to use the name Barton when signing the register.

In our room I took Hazel to the window and showed her the lights of the casino. "Does that mean you're going sky-hooting off on your own now?" she inquired.

"I've got to find out what's happened since I left here," I explained. "Don't break the bank at the first sitting. It's not considered good form." I thought of something. "Don't go broke, either. We'd play hell getting an infusion of fresh cash here under your current pseudonym." I kissed the tip of her nose and left the room.

I took a cab to Rawson Square. One of the oddities about Nassau at night is the absence of neon. What lighting exists is subdued, which didn't make me unhappy as I walked to Eurydice Street. There was a light on behind the window lettered Chen Yi's Massage Parlor as I approached it, but I tried the door leading upstairs to Candy's apartment.

It opened, and I slipped inside, then used the side door entrance to the massage parlor, bypassing its tiny waiting room. Female voices came from one of the curtained cubicles. I hesitated. I didn't want to bother Chen Yi while she was at work, but I didn't feel I had a lot of time to waste.

While I was debating how I was going to get her attention, the curtain parted, and Chen Yi herself emerged. The tall Chinese girl was wearing a short-sleeved, short-skirted white uniform that gave her the hygienic appearance of a nurse.

She stopped short at the sight of me. "No one is permitted back here without an attendant," she said coldly.

I had expected her to recognize me. I had forgotten my changed appearance. When she advanced toward me to emphasize her statement, I backed away rapidly, knowing that physically she was a match for me in any department. "It's me," I said.

By that time she had me backed into the reception area. Her expression changed. "You're not—"

I unbuttoned my jacket, then undid the top two buttons on my shirt. I plucked my undershirt far enough away from my body so Chen Yi could see my chest. She stared at the patchwork of scars she had seen before where skin had been removed to rebuild my face, then took my chin in her right hand, and studied my made-up face carefully. "I still wouldn't believe it if it were not for the voice," she said softly.

"What happened?" I asked.

"Quietly," she said in an undertone and beckoned me to follow her. She led me to the last massage booth as I tiptoed after her. She drew the curtain and turned on a small table radio that rested on a cabinet top crowded with towels, creams, liniments, and body oils. The sound of calypso music filled the booth.

The Chinese girl pointed in the direction of the occupied booth. "Hermione," she said softly. "I blame her for what happened." Her smile was savage. "I spend my time planning things for Hermione."

"What happened? Where's Candy?"

"Hospitalized. From a syndicate beating."

I could hear my own indrawn breath. "Bad?"

"At first the doctor feared for the sight of one eye, but there has been an improvement."

"But Candy didn't know I'd been into syndicate affairs!" I protested. "Neither did I until he came back from downtown that morning with the word the safe deposit boxes had been syndicate property."

"He was beaten because he had made no effort to find out where you had hidden the material taken from the safe deposit boxes before you left Nassau. They expected him to be more curious in their behalf."

"I guess that makes me the villain," I said awkwardly.

She shook her dark head. "He doesn't blame you. He considers it another poor hand in a run of bad cards." She hesitated for a second. "There is something I should tell you. When I spoke to him yesterday, Candy said that of the two of you he was the lucky one because they'd left him alive."

There wasn't anything I could say to that. Somehow the might of the syndicate had seemed an intangible thing until I thought of the rocklike, seemingly indestructible Candy hospitalized. For one of the few times in my life I felt a cold thrill along my spine.

"Why are you here?" Chen Yi's voice brought me back to the present.

"You know why I'm here."

"Stubborn," she said. "Foolishly stubborn. Yet—"

"What?"

"I wish I could help." She said it with every evidence of sincerity. "I would do anything to frustrate them." She continued on without a break. "I learned this afternoon that your friend was still at Cartwright Street."

So the trip hadn't been for nothing. I pointed toward the ceiling. "D'you want to help badly enough to let me stay in Candy's apartment?"

Her eyes widened, and for an instant her expression became almost gleeful. "How clever! The one place they would never think of looking. I've been there only briefly since Candy—since Candy—" She didn't finish it.

"Then you'll let me?"

She nodded. "I will move back in. Under the circumstances I believe Candy would want you to and would think it a fine joke." Her dark eyes became shadowed again. "Although I won't tell him about it now."

"I'm not alone," I said.

I don't know how she knew, but her understanding smile had a Mona Lisa aspect to it. "She will be most welcome," the Chinese girl said. "Bring her before dawn. And be careful on the streets. Your appearance is changed, but they have not given up. You will—"

"Hey, Chen Yi!" a feminine voice I recognized as Hermione's called from the end booth. "How about getting this gunk off me and getting me ready for my date with Arnold?"

"Coming!" Chen Yi responded, then lowered her voice. "Be careful. Please. I don't wish to see again what I was forced to witness."

"We'll be back in a couple of hours," I said. "And thanks."

Chen Yi led me to the side door, and this time I heard the snick of its lock after she let me out into the dimly lit street with its row of whitewashed buildings.

EIGHT

I FOUND Hazel at the roulette wheel in the Paradise Island Hotel casino.

At first glance there appeared to be more casino employees present than gamblers. The roulette wheel area in particular wasn't overcrowded. Two women in evening dress and an elderly man in a dinner jacket made up half the customers. Then there was a lone male with thick spectacles smoking a foul-smelling cigarette in a foot-long holder, and a younger woman with an expensive fur thrown carelessly over her shoulders.

And Hazel.

I sat down next to her. She had four stacks of different colored chips in front of her, and she gave me a quick smile while pushing in my direction a double stack of black chips with gold rims. "Nobody can seem to get untracked here," she said. "See what you can do." She picked up a handful of rust chips and placed three each on fourteen through nineteen.

I watched the spin of the ivory ball in the track inside the wheel as the croupier started it with the casual-looking flick of the wrist they practice for hours. All the gamblers except Hazel had notebooks beside them in which they jotted down the results of each spin. The ivory ball descended from the rim and click clacked out of the wheel's numbered boxes before coming to rest in seventeen. The impassive-faced croupier swept the marker board clean with his little rake except for Hazel's seventeen. He returned her 105 chips for her 3.

Hazel doubled her bet on fourteen through nineteen. The only thing I know about roulette is that if the wheel has a double zero, the percentage is stacked too highly in favor of the house. This wheel had a double zero. I took one of the stacks of chips Hazel had given me and pushed it onto the square of green baize that gave me a winner with any of the even numbers on the wheel. Across the board from me the man with the cigarette holder scattered chips with lordly disdain and apparent aimlessness.

The ivory ball clacked down into twenty-two. Hazel was wiped out, but Cigarette Holder had a winner. The croupier doubled my stack of chips on the even, and I pushed them back onto the odd. Twenty-nine came up, and he doubled my stack again. I pushed it all back onto the even, and it came up four.

I moved the eight-times augmented stack onto the odd again. "We've got to get out of here," I muttered to Hazel from the corner of my mouth. The ivory ball settled into fifteen, and the croupier doubled my chips again.

I became aware that one of the women in evening dress was staring at me as I shoved the mound of chips onto the even marker. *"Faites vos jeux, mesdames et messieurs,"* the croupier droned, and the woman hurriedly dropped a single chip on the same twenty-eight she had been backing steadily.

Twelve came up. "You want to leave right now?" Hazel asked in a tone of voice the table could hear. The croupier measured out stacks of chips as he doubled mine.

"One more spin," I said, and pushed the thirty-two-times augmented pile of chips onto the odd again. The ivory ball settled into double zero. "My mother told me there'd be nights like this," I said as the croupier raked the board clean. I took the second stack of chips Hazel had given me, removed one, and handed her the rest. "Cash in, doll."

While she was at the cashier's cage, I walked to the casino entrance and asked the doorman to get us a cab. It was waiting when Hazel rejoined me, and I gave the black doorman the single chip I'd retained from Hazel's stack. He ran to the cab solicitously and opened its door, then bowed us in. He did everything but kneel on the ground. "What the hell was that chip worth I just gave him?" I asked Hazel as the cab pulled away.

I had a glimpse of her face in the light of the marquee. She was laughing so hard she couldn't speak. "What's so damned funny, woman?"

"You—are!" she got out between sputtered giggles. "The—last of the big spenders!"

I punched her in the ribs. "What was that chip worth?"

"Where to, sair?" the driver inquired.

"Rawson Square." I returned my attention to Hazel. "What was the chip worth?" I repeated.

"Twenty dollars."

"Twenty—oh, no! How many chips were in that first stack I played?"

She shrugged. "Ten or twelve."

"Holy cow! Even if it was ten—" Mentally I reviewed the progression of my five winning bets. The stake was $200, then $400, $800, $1600, $3200 and $6400. I thought of the mound of chips swallowed up by the double zero. "You mean you let me fall off for $12,800 without saying a word?"

"You were doing so nicely, dear." Hazel said. She giggled again. "The croupier was about to invoke a limit after the fifth spin until he heard what I said about leaving. Then he was afraid you'd get offended and draw down all of it if he imposed a limit."

"Which I damn well would have if I'd known what was involved, and I wouldn't have had to be offended, either."

"I thought you had decided to ignore your own rule

about not breaking the bank at the first sitting." In the light of a streetlight I could see Hazel's wide smile.

"The kind of banks I used to do business with didn't have double zeros to save them," I informed her. The cab drew up across the street from the hackney stand in Rawson Square. "We walk from here."

I helped Hazel from the cab after paying off the driver. She walked along beside me with her free-swinging stride, breathing deeply of the flower-scented Bahamian night. "What's the occasion for this expedition?" she asked.

"I've found us a better place to stay." I almost said safer, but at the last second I kept it off my tongue.

Hazel glanced around curiously at the white-washed buildings and shops on Eurydice Street. "It looks like a picture postcard of a Moroccan native quarter," she remarked. "Does everyone here grow flowers?"

"It's the national pastime." We were approaching Candy's apartment, and I steered Hazel to the massage parlor entrance. "Here we are." The door was locked and I rang the bell.

Chen Yi appeared in her white uniform and opened the door. I pointed to the cubicle where Hermione had been, my eyebrows raised in a voiceless question. "She is gone," Chen Yi said in her soft voice. "I am alone here now."

Hazel was studying the room and the curtained cubicles. "Chen Yi, this is Hazel," I introduced them. The two women eyed each other cautiously. For one of the few times in her life Hazel had to look upward at another woman. "I've told Hazel everything except that Candy is away for a few days," I said to the Chinese girl. She nodded understandingly. "You two go upstairs, and I'll be along in a few minutes."

Chen Yi's look was inquiring, but I didn't elaborate. Having been on the street in that neighborhood twice already that night, I wanted to spend five minutes surveying the area from behind the massage parlor curtains to assure myself that nobody was taking an undue interest in the fact.

"I will lock up for the night then," Chen Yi said and began turning out the lights. When she had left only a night light burning on the rear wall and had relocked the front door, she turned to Hazel. "If you will come with me, please."

She shepherded Hazel to the side door which led the way to the stairway to Candy's apartment. I waited for a good ten minutes in the massage parlor, scanning the street through a narrow space between the draperies. There was no sign of unusual activity, so I climbed the stairs to join the ladies after a final look around.

Chen Yi threw over the bar bolt when I rang at the upstairs door and admitted me. Hazel was right behind her, and there had been a metamorphosis. Both were wearing beautiful identical Chinese hostess gowns. Hazel and Chen Yi looked like sorority sisters or members of the same tong. Hazel's flaming red hair was even piled up on top of her head in imitation of Chen Yi's elaborate, raven hairdo.

Hazel bowed low to me with her arms folded and her hands hidden in the loose, flowing folds of each opposite sleeve. She began to chant in a singsong voice, and Chen Yi smiled appreciatively. "I learned a few childrens' songs from the Chinese farmers who worked our ranch garden when I was a child," Hazel explained to me. "What about our bags?"

"I'll have them sent to the massage parlor in the morning. It would have caused too many people to take notice if we'd checked out completely at the hotel tonight."

We went into the kitchen, and Chen Yi and Hazel prepared a meal. In some manner I couldn't understand, the two women seemed to have achieved instant rapport. I felt very much relieved as we sat down to a tasty meal of fried rice, boned chicken, and Chinese vegetables. If they liked each other, it was going to make my situation a lot easier.

There was no dessert, but Chen Yi served green tea in the Incense Room. "What is your home like?" she asked Hazel when we all had cigarettes lighted.

"It's in a mountain valley," Hazel replied. She drew a flat circle in the air with her finger and then made a heaping motion with her hands as if piling up the hills on either side. "Sixty-four hundred feet high. Very hot sun and very dry air, but the valleys have water. Just two free-flowing springs in Ely supply water for the entire community. All the ranches have never-fail dug wells."

"It sounds like the southern part of Taiwan," Chen Yi murmured. She took a sip of her tea before she spoke again. "You wish to speak of what must be done?" she asked me directly.

"Not tonight," I said firmly. "We'll talk in the morning. Tonight I intend to sleep."

And when Chen Yi showed us to a bedroom, not even Hazel's wiliest blandishments, which ultimately took the form of a Chinese strip tease, were enough to change my mind.

Chen Yi and I had coffee together in the morning. Hazel was still asleep. I had planned the questions I wanted to ask the Chinese girl while taking my shower. "You had better eat," she said before I could begin, and I waited while she fixed and served eggs and toast.

She sat across the table from me with her dark eyes upon my face. "Have you heard anything about my partner while I've been away?" I asked.

"No. But I've divided my time almost entirely between the business and the hospital. It's possible there have been developments I haven't learned."

I felt that the next question was the crux of the entire matter. I phrased it carefully. "Do you recall after I left here whether you and Candy happened to mention in Hermione's hearing that my partner was in the local jail?"

"I don't remember," Chen Yi said slowly. "I—it's possible that we did. We didn't know—certainly I had no idea at that time—how dangerous it was to speak loosely in Hermione's presence because of her tale bearing to her gangster friend. It didn't even occur to me until those men came to brutalize Candy." She nodded her head several times in rapid succession. "Yes, I see why you have returned to Nassau. If the syndicate knows that your friend is there—"

"How easy would it be for them to get at him?"

"I'm sorry, but I don't know. Candy would know."

"You visit him every day?"

"Yes."

"Is he in good enough condition that you could ask him? Without mentioning me?" I didn't want Candy concerned about the extent of Chen Yi's involvement.

"I think so. In fact I'm sure so. Is there anything else I can do?"

I was ready for the query. "Two things. First, while I'm at the Paradise Island Hotel this morning arranging for our bags to be brought to your shop downstairs, could you inquire if the American is still being held in jail here? It wouldn't make much sense for me to lay on something if he'd already been transferred."

"I can do that easily when I go downtown this morning. What is his name?"

It stopped me. Certainly the name wouldn't be Erikson. "There wouldn't be more than one American held there, would there? Other than an overnight drunk?"

"Possibly not. It seems unlikely. What is the second thing you wish me to do?"

"Something a bit more difficult. I've already learned that the tough part of any plan will be getting my partner off the island. I'm thinking now of getting him first to one of the Out Islands. Andros, Bimini, and Eleuthera all have airports where he might be able to get a private plane to take him to Florida. Or I'm sure he can make some other arrangement if I get him that far. Can you get in touch with a boatman with something seaworthy enough to make a quick run to one of those islands?"

"It's not as difficult as you feared. There is a man I can ask who is knowledgeable about such things. Candy has used him. I'm almost sure he can direct me to someone who will have the right kind of vessel."

"Fine. You realize that you'll have to have a reason for asking?"

"I'll say that Candy and I are going on a vacation." She reflected for a moment. "To a place on one of the islands where the direct ferry service couldn't take us."

"That should do it." I rephrased my next question three times mentally before I came out with it. "You realize that there's a chance the syndicate might learn you're helping me?"

"It doesn't matter." She said it with no particular emphasis, but there was a smoldering light in her dark eyes. "Every time I think of those four brutes beating Candy while he tried not to let me know how much they were hurting him—" Her voice died away momentarily. "He wouldn't defend himself, and he wouldn't let me do anything because he was afraid of what they'd do to me." There was a faraway look in her eyes. "I have heard my father speak of methods for dealing with such carrion," she said and then appeared to come back to the present. "Are we ready for me to go now?"

"I think so. Be careful."

"If you leave before I come back, be sure and have your woman throw the bar on the door."

"I'll do that."

"I like Hazel," Chen Yi said. "There is no pretense about her. You are a fortunate man."

"I'll play that contract vulnerable and redoubled," I agreed. Chen Yi removed her shopping bag from behind the kitchen door. "Be careful. These are not nice people."

"I would like to have the chance to show them that

neither am I," she said. "I find Hermione incredible. She evidently relates no cause and effect between her tale bearing and what happened to Candy. How she can blithely return here for a massage in the face of what she did I fail to understand. I spoke to Candy about refusing to have her here, but he said no."

"I've been meaning to ask you ever since the first night I was here," I said. "When you and Candy were on the wrestling mat, I recognized the judo, but what is this gung fu?"

"It's not meant for an exhibition or a contest," Chen Yi said. "It's intended to cripple or kill. It's difficult to practice for that reason. I learned it from my brothers whom my father had instructed as children." She walked to the door at the head of the stairs, and I followed. "I should be back in an hour," she said.

I threw the bar over on the door, then went into the bedroom, and woke Hazel. That Amazon sat up and sleepily knuckled her eyes. "Where's Chen Yi?" she asked.

"Out marketing. And I'm going over to the hotel to get our bags transferred. Come on out here with me. I want to show you how this door works."

Hazel padded after me to the head of the stairs, her full-fleshed nudity almost distracting me from my purpose. I demonstrated the swing-over movement of the bar which lodged its business end in a steel-lined slot deep in the wall, then pointed out the one-way glass which permitted a view of whoever was standing on the other side of the door. "Don't open it for anyone but Chen Yi or me," I warned Hazel. "I won't be long."

I opened the door and started down the stairs before she could ask questions. I stood near the top until I heard the snick of the locking bar, then waved to the one-way glass, and finished the descent.

There was no problem at the hotel. "My wife and I are under doctor's orders to receive deep massage for our arthritic problems," I said casually to the desk clerk while he was making out the bill. It was probably wasted effort, since he didn't appear to be listening. I accepted my change, tipped the bell captain who was going to handle the transfer, and walked from Paradise Island back across the bridge to downtown Nassau.

I was tempted to walk past the detention cells on Cartwright Street to look for possible problems there, but I decided to wait until Chen Yi had made her report. If Erikson had been moved elsewhere for any reason, I'd have to start from scratch again.

I took a zigzag route back to Eurydice Street, checking out construction jobs in the area. To free Karl Erikson, I needed tools and explosives, and the easiest place—perhaps the only place on this small island—to come by the proper kinds of both at the same spot would be at a construction site.

I had seen three construction jobs on Paradise Island, at least one of which was a hotel, but none had had a red-flagged explosives shack near their locked tool sheds. And something closer to Candy's apartment would be much better since I'd have to tote the stuff myself.

There was plenty of construction going on in the Rawson Square area but again no explosives shacks. Evidently the island's substance below ground level didn't require much blasting. I was going to have to cast my nets a little wider to come up with something suitable.

Chen Yi and Hazel both answered the door at the apartment when I rang. They were in identical Chinese costume again, and Chen Yi had been attempting to put Hazel's hair up in the same graceful, fanlike style I had always seen Chen Yi wearing, except during her wrestling mat practice with Candy. At that time her long hair had streamed down her back.

"My hair is too short," Hazel lamented. "I'm going to have to grow it longer to wear it like Chen Yi does. Don't you think it would be sensational?"

"I think it's pretty damn sensational the way it is, baby."

"A master of the soft answer," Chen Yi smiled. She led the way into the Incense Room, and we all sat down on the low divans circling it. Hazel and I were together on one divan, Chen Yi across from us. She crossed her arms and rested each palm flat on the opposite thigh, looking like a statue in a Chinese pagoda. "I'm afraid what I learned isn't going to be of too much help," she said, coming directly to the point.

"What's the trouble?"

"There are two Americans being held at Cartwright Street. They are in cells three and four, they are not tourists or seamen, and they have not been officially charged yet, so there is no other information."

"It's funny my partner hasn't been charged yet," I commented. "Although some jurisdictions like to check out the identity first." And they'd have a fine time trying to check out Karl Erikson's. "But I see what you mean. With no charge on the books you weren't able to find out if either of the men being held is my partner."

"That is correct," Chen Yi agreed. "And my informant had seen neither."

"Have you ever seen the inside of the detention setup at Cartwright Street, Chen Yi?"

She nodded. "Once I bailed Candy out after a gambling inquiry—" she smiled briefly "—what you call a raid."

"Do you remember the arrangement of the cells?"

"Surely. They are in a long line against the back wall of the building."

"That's the best news I've had today." If I could just find out which cell held Erikson and its position in relation to the back of the building, I doubted that I'd have too much trouble getting him out of it when the time came. "What about the boat to get him away from here?"

"A man is coming to see me here tonight. You can decide if he's suitable."

"We're rolling," I said and stood up and stretched. "I'm going to flake out for a bit." I didn't say so, but I knew I had a busy evening coming up. "Wake me at four, will you?" I said to Hazel.

"Do you want lunch now?" she asked.

"When I get up," I decided. I went into the bedroom, leaving the two women together. I took off my shoes and my jacket and stretched out on the bed. I didn't really expect to fall asleep, but I did.

I woke with a start to find Hazel shaking me. I had a knot on my arm where I'd slept on my shoulder holster. "It's four o'clock," she said. "Chen Yi is back from the hospital."

"How's Candy coming along?" I asked before I remembered that Hazel wasn't supposed to know anything about Candy.

"Improving," Hazel said. She sat down on the edge of the bed. "You didn't tell me the syndicate had put Candy in the hospital, Earl. No, don't blame Chen Yi. All she told me at first was that she had to go out for awhile, but the moment I saw the pains she was taking in dressing herself, I knew. I'd thought from the beginning that it was curious that Candy wasn't here, so I wormed the truth out of her."

I really didn't blame Chen Yi; I'd had personal experience with that suction pump of Hazel's once she had it working. And Chen Yi's openness with Hazel was just another indication of their quick recognition of each other as basically the same sort of people. "I'm glad to hear he's coming along," I said.

"This is really dangerous, isn't it, Earl?" Hazel continued. She spoke quietly, but she placed her hand on mine. "I'm just beginning to appreciate the danger."

"I'd call it more complicated than dangerous," I objected. "Diddling both the syndicate boys and the local police could get a bit involved, but I hope to make it a hit-and-run job that will have us all out of here before anyone realizes what's going on. There's nothing—"

There was a tap on the bedroom door. "Come in, Chen Yi," Hazel said.

The Chinese girl came into the room. "I asked Candy how he sized up your partner's position," she said gravely to me. "He felt that it was only a question of time before the syndicate reached him. He believed that the only reason they hadn't already was because they hesitated to create an overt incident which would turn the heat on them locally." She paused. "I thought you'd want to know."

"Thanks," I said, sitting up on the bed and feeling for my shoes with my toes. I pulled them on and laced them. "This job will be a piece of cake compared to some," I continued as much for effect upon Hazel as Chen Yi. "I'm going out for half an hour, so how about postponing that lunch till I get back?"

"I'll have it ready," Hazel said. Her big arms wrapped around me as I reached for my jacket. "Please be careful. Please?"

"You know it, Sugarfoot."

I left the apartment.

What I had in mind was a quick trip to Cartwright Street to look over the jail building in daylight. I'd already decided after hearing Chen Yi's transmission of Candy's estimate of the situation that if I ran into no unusual problems on this scouting expedition and on the project I planned for later tonight, I'd tell Chen Yi to have her boatman stand by for tomorrow night. In view of what Candy had said, it could be dangerous to string it out.

Cartwright Street dozed gently in the Bahamian sunlight. By US standards the jail building was almost indistinguishable from its neighbors, but I recognized it from Candy's description. From the front it could have been anything: doctor's office, lawyer's, architect's. Whatever the original color of its bricked-over exterior, it had been roasted to a dull dun color by that constant Bahamian sun.

I turned the corner and walked along one side. In depth the building extended only partway back into the block. A narrow alley ran behind it with a weatherbeaten, six-foot-high board fence separating the building line from the alley. The back of the building was a good dozen feet away from the fence, I noted with satisfaction. It guaranteed sufficient working room.

I strolled through the alley. Through a knothole I could see barred windows, the bottom edges of which were at least six feet above the ground. My view was so fuzzy I couldn't get a real sense of the building's construction. There didn't appear to be any glass in the windows. The even-tempered Bahamian climate probably precluded the necessity and provided for whatever ventilation was needed inside.

I straightened up from the knothole and looked around me. There was no one in the alley except me. There was no noise in the neighborhood. I took two running strides, grabbed the top of the fence in both hands, and swung myself over it.

I landed in soft sand and knee-deep bunch grass. There was still no sound. I scrambled erect and quickly approached the building, flattening myself against it so I couldn't be seen from inside. The first close-up look at the hoked-up masonry construction convinced me that the only problem in blasting Erikson out of there would be to fashion a charge minimal enough that it wouldn't flatten the building and everyone in it. Except for the bars it looked as though a little solid heel-and-toe work would have been sufficient.

I studied the barred windows. Which of them was Karl Erikson behind? Chen Yi had said the two Americans were in cells three and four. No matter whether the cells were numbered from left to right or from right to left, cells three and four were the two middle cells in the six-cell lineup. But which one was Erikson in? I wasn't going to get two chances when it came time to lower the boom.

I backed away from the building into the shade of the fence. The accumulated building heat must have made the jail's interior almost intolerable. When I put a hand on the fence, I noticed a loose board almost ready to come off. I moved a couple of feet away, pulled myself up to the top of it, balanced precariously, then slowly straightened up. I was almost at the same level as the barred windows.

"I say theah!" The sound of the indignant voice almost shocked me off the fence. "You're not permitted up theah, you know!"

I focused on a black face in a uniform inside the fourth cell from the right. The jailer had a tray of food in his hands, and he was looking out through the bars at me. More important, though, over his shoulder I saw a shock of blond hair that could only belong to Karl Erikson.

I dropped down from the fence to the dusty alley, then walked rapidly up the alley and around the corner and around the next two corners before slowing down. My heartbeat gradually slowed down from its adrenalin-paced thumping. Despite the scare the mission had been successful.

If I had any decent sort of luck tonight in seeking the material I needed, and if Chen Yi's boatman measured up at all, we were getting close to the critical moment.

I walked back to Candy's apartment in a much better frame of mind.

NINE

HAZEL opened the door for me. "How did it go?" she asked.

"Fine. He's still there."

She led the way into the kitchen. Chen Yi was pouring fresh-brewed tea over a jam of ice in tall glasses. Hazel went to the stove and began dishing up something I couldn't identify but which smelled delicious. "Guess what Chen Yi and I have been doing?" she said.

"What?"

"Exchanging tricks."

"In bed?" I said, pretending to be shocked.

Hazel and Chen Yi both laughed. "Don't be giving us ideas," Hazel replied. "No, she was showing me a couple of her *gung fu* tactics." Hazel shook her head. "Real cripplers."

"And you were showing her?"

"My roll-of-nickels-in-the-handkerchief gimmick."

I knew the gimmick. Hazel always carried a roll of nickels loosely wrapped in a handkerchief in a separate compartment of her handbag. She can get it out with the handkerchief draped to conceal the roll and to protect her knuckles as fast as I can draw my gun, and with the weight of her healthy hundred-fifty-pounds behind a smash to the jaw she generates about four less horsepower than it takes to drop a steer. "So what did you finally decide?" I asked.

"We each still like our own." Hazel motioned to the table. "Sit down. We've eaten already."

I pulled a chair up to the table and dumped two teaspoons of sugar into my tea and churned the ice around with a tall spoon until moisture dotted the sides of the glass. Hazel and Chen Yi sat down at the table, too. I glanced at Chen Yi who sat pensively with her beautiful face cupped in the joined palms of her hands. "If your boatman measures up, we're in good shape," I told her between bites of a spicy mixture of meat and vegetables.

"Why don't I call him now so you can speak to him and reassure yourself on that point?" she asked.

"I'd rather meet him personally than speak to him on the phone," I said. "Is it safe for him to come here, or should I meet him somewhere else?"

"There's no reason why it shouldn't be here," she replied. "He visits Candy occasionally." She rose to her feet. "I'll call him now and ask him to come. He's Australian, not young, but Candy says he's reliable." She started toward the telephone in the hallway. "His name is Hurricane Ronnie," she called back over her shoulder.

Hazel was smiling when she looked at me. "With a name like Hurricane Ronnie what more do you need to know about him?"

"Chen Yi said he's not young," I pointed out. "I'd like to make sure he's not covered with barnacles."

She placed her hand on top of mine with a sigh. "All this seems so—so unreal. I still can't picture Karl Erikson cooped up in a jail cell."

"He's there all right. At least I'm sure now that he hasn't been shipped out to a penal camp on Dry Tortugas." I thought about it for a minute. "What I don't understand is why he's still there at all, unless my original hunch is correct and nobody knows he's in trouble. With the connections he has in Washington, if anyone knew he was there, I just have to think he'd have been out of there before now, either by the front or back door."

"But didn't you say that on every job you've done with him he made a point of telling you that you were strictly on your own and couldn't look for help if anything went wrong?" Hazel said in a questioning tone.

"That's part of the drill, Hazel. And behind the Iron Curtain it might hold good, although even then with limitations. But with a friendly power involved things can be arranged."

"What kind of things?"

"Requests at high levels, a bit of financial pressure, an offer of tit for tat. That sort of thing. It's more true of us than it is of the Europeans. They have a much longer history of professionalism than we do. But even that's changing. Captured spies are swapped now. Look at England's swap of Gordon Lonsdale for Greville Wynne. A very bad bargain on their part. Almost as bad as some of the exchanges we've made in handing over top flight professionals for comparatively valueless agents."

I took a long swallow from my glass, letting the clear ice cubes slide down and press their cold wetness against my upper lip. "There's usually not much publicity about it, but look at the way this country operates. The US of A, I mean. Agencies bend over backward to rescue an individual. Quietly of course, except in wartime. Then miles of ocean or of jungle are combed to find a downed flyer."

"But Karl is still in jail here," Hazel commented.

"Because they don't know he's here. Or because the wheels are turning beneath the surface. If it wasn't for the syndicate involvement, he'd be having the equivalent of a rest cure."

Chen Yi reentered the kitchen as I was cleaning up my plate. "He will be here in an hour," she promised.

"Good. Where's our cigarettes, Hazel?"

"In the bedroom." She followed me there. "What happens after you get Karl out?" she asked me.

"Thanks for the positive statement. What happens with us, you mean? We'll just take off like the nice little tourists we are. We'll take the first plane out of here to a nice quiet spot and sit back for a couple of weeks and relax and enjoy ourselves. Erikson will have to go to Washington, and I wish him luck there. I'm going to do him this one favor for old time's sake and because he once fished you out of the drink at a critical moment. But from now on I hope our only contact is via Christmas card every fifth year."

Hazel removed from my hand the cigarette I'd taken from the pack on the dresser. Then she slowly unbuttoned the top three buttons on my shirt. "Chen Yi said he wouldn't be here for an hour," she murmured.

I removed my shoulder holster so she could take off my shirt. She unbelted my trousers and lowered them, then peeled down my shorts. I sat down on the bed and took off my shoes while Hazel stripped in swirling flashes of color in which pale, silky white came more and more to predominate. She joined me on the bed.

A friend told me once that the best piece he ever had in his life was ten minutes after he got out of a jam so bad he should never have walked away alive. He had a theory that the survival of danger or the anticipation of danger turned on a man's adrenalin. He could have been right. The little scare I'd had at the jail building and/or the thought of acquiring the materials that night that I needed for the jailbreak seemed to have perked mine up. Hazel had no difficulty in turning it to her immediate advantage.

We rolled together on the bed and fitted ourselves into the intricate but natural groove. I had a bigger head of steam up than I thought, even; I pounded her until I thought my eyeballs would fall out. Beneath me Hazel vocalized in wordless rivulets of sound. Her big arms held me so tightly that we were riveted together chest to chest. We came down the stretch together stride for stride and tripped the photo-finish electric beam in a near dead heat.

I must have fallen asleep afterward, because the next thing I knew Hazel was shaking me. "Hurricane Ronnie is here," she said. She was dressed again.

"How does he look?" I asked as I scrambled into my clothes.

"Wait till you see him," she said, and that was all I could get out of her. She patted my arm when I finished dressing. "You're not in such bad shape for a rather elderly sex maniac," she said.

I pinched her where she wouldn't show it in Sunday school. "You should have had it when it was good," I told her. We both smiled. She knew she'd had it when it was at its best.

I picked up my holster automatically, then dropped it on the bed. Then I changed my mind, picked it up again, and slipped into it. This Australian boat captain was a critical piece in the puzzle. If he was going to back off at the sight of a .38 in a shoulder holster, it was a lot better to have him do it right now.

We went into the Incense Room. Chen Yi was sitting on a divan with the room's only other occupant, and for a second I thought the two women were putting me on. The man with Chen Yi must have been on the far side of fifty, but it was hard to be sure because a great mop of thick gray hair came to his shoulders and a Moses-type beard concealed most of his face. A long, narrow nose peered forth from the aurora of hairy growth, and above the nose very light blue, mischievous eyes gave the first indication there might be more to the package than appearances indicated.

Appearance certainly didn't indicate much. Hurricane Ronnie was attired in a short-sleeved, red-and-white, horizontally striped jersey and white duck trousers cut off raggedly just below the knees. The white ducks were supported precariously by a multicolored scarf that served as a belt. Thin, bare arms and legs were mahogany brown from constant exposure to the tropical sun. They were also corded with lean muscles that hinted at wiry strength. The leather sandals he wore were so nearly the color of his suntanned feet that at first I thought he was barefoot.

He rose from the divan with hand extended. I felt the rasp of dry callouses against my palm. "Cap'n Ronald Firbank at y'r service, myte," he said in a scratchy voice with a pronounced Anglo-Australian accent. "Nymed for the bleedin' novelist, no less, by a soft-in-the-'ead mother. I understand, guv'nor, you've a need for quick and quiet transport. I've a bloody fine crawft to place at your disposal if we caun reach a satisfact'ry agreement."

He was still holding my hand, and his little birdlike eyes were fixed upon my shoulder holster. "I see you don't wear that for show, myte," he continued.

"You haven't seen the gun," I countered, "so how do you know it's not for show?"

"I've no need to see the gun," he declared, finally dropping my hand. "I can see the sweat stains an' creases which tell an hinterested observer like meself that you wear the thing like your own bloody pelt." The facial hair parted amidships to reveal stained yellow teeth in a surprisingly small-boyish smile. "So what's the caper, guv'nor?"

There was no sense in holding back. "I'm going to take an inmate out of the back end of the jail here tonight, and you're going to transfer him on your boat to a nearby island with an airstrip."

The blue eyes were unwavering. "A hinterestin' proposition, guv'nor. A damned hinterestin' proposition. I don't mind tellin' you strictly man to man that I've spent a few short periods in that same jyle as a unwillin' guest of the Hestablishment, an' it'd give me aright fair amount o' pleasure to put a fly in their dish o' marmalade."

Behind the Australian Chen Yi and Hazel were nodding their heads in identical fashion. Evidently Hurricane Ronnie had earned the feminine seal of approval. And I had long ago learned to trust Hazel's intuition more than my own. "What kind of boat do you have available?"

"Eight ton o' solid oak, guv'nor. No yacht, y' unner-stand. She was a two-sticker once, but I lost one in a storm when I was playin' mailboat after the guv'ment boat refused to try it. She's a jury-rigged jib an' mains'l job now but with a reliable auxiliary. She'll still do twelve knots anywhere in the Islands from West End on Grand Bahama to Matthew Town on Great Inagua."

"Where would you suggest taking him?"

"Eleuthera," he said confidently. "There's an airport has commercial flights at its north end, an' if the gold's available, I shouldn't wonder he could charter if necessary."

"And the price?" He looked at me. "Your price?"

"Well, now we're gettin' down t' the meat of't." The blue eyes closed while Hurricane Ronnie cogitated. "Considerin' the circumstances, guv'nor, I'd say five hundred for the ship rental an' five hundred for the passenger."

"Does that include your help behind the jail if I should happen to need it?"

"That's the package." Hurricane Ronnie winked. "Tell you the truth, if I was sure of gettin' in a tug or two there where the hair was a bit short, I'd be tempted to cut m' price a little."

Hazel handed me her handbag while the stringy little boatman looked at her with approval. I counted out two stacks of money on the low coffee table. "Here's five hundred for the boat. The other five hundred you collect from Chen Yi after delivering the passenger."

"Fair enough, guv'nor. Couldn't be fairer." He picked up one stack of bills and stuffed them into a pocket of the ragged white ducks.

"Now what about a plan? Where will you be moored?"

"Let's tyke first things first, guv'nor," Hurricane Ronnie replied. The feel of the money in his pocket seemed to have put him in an expansive mood. "First dog out o' the box, there's but one proper time to jerk your man out. Not before 2:00 A.M. an' not later than 2:30."

"That's a tight schedule," I objected.

He nodded, bushy whiskers bristling. "But a reasonable one, myte. That's the hour the night shift bobbies tyke their tea. Things 're a bit higgledy-piggledy around the jyle durin' that interval. Oh, the bobbies'll react, all right, but shall we say not with bags of enthusiasm?"

"And then?"

"Whuff-whuff t' the good ship *Matilda*."

"At the marina?"

"Not at the marina, guv'nor. For the short tyme we'll need to be there I'll tie up at the out end o' pier nine, right next t' the wharf where the Commonwealth Fuel an' Petroleum Warehouse stands. There's no tankers or freighters due in for three dyes, an' the only crawft along that section of pier 'll be the tug an' barge that hauls petrol an' lubricants to the Out Islands. There'll be plenty o' room for me to slip the *Matilda* in, an' it'll be the last place the jolly old police 'd think of lookin' for a fishin' smack."

"How far from the jail to pier nine?"

"Seven or eight minutes by car. Ten at the most." Hurricane Ronnie looked at me quizzically. "You do 'ave a car, myte? You've bloody well got to 'ave one to swing the deal. No hother way we could move fast enough."

I looked at the silent Chen Yi. "How did he get here?"

"He has a truck," she said. "Not of much worth."

I returned my attention to the little boat captain. "So it seems I have transportation."

"For a slight hadditional consideration," he agreed amiably.

I counted out another thousand dollars and again split it into two piles. A calloused hand picked up one pile and stuffed it away with the first bundle. "Leave the truck here when you go," I told him. I'd have need of it soon.

The truck was a real windfall. "Off the street somewhere. Where can he park it, Chen Yi?"

"Behind the shop," she said. She made a circle in the air with one finger to indicate the direction. Hurricane Ronnie nodded.

"Are we straight now?" I asked him.

"Righto, myte. I'll berth the *Matilda* at one fifteen an' meet you in the alley behind the jail a half hour lyter. But park the truck a little bit away, right? Then we'll spring the lad an' tickety-boo it for the *Matilda*." He paused. "Which night are we layin' it on?"

It was my turn to pause. I thought of Candy's warning as transmitted by Chen Yi about the syndicate's obsession with getting to Erikson. Why delay if I had any success in obtaining what I needed to get him out? "Would tonight be too soon?"

"Not a bit," he said promptly.

"Or tomorrow night," I amended it. "Can Chen Yi call you to let you know?" Both Chen Yi and Hurricane Ronnie nodded. "Good." I took a crisp hundred dollar bill from Hazel's bag and placed it on the coffee table. "You can take that along with you, too, if you can tell me where on the island there's any explosives stored. On one of the construction jobs, I mean. Dynamite or plastique preferably."

"Now that's tricky stuff, guv'nor," the bewhiskered boat captain said slowly. He picked up the bill and studied both sides of it longingly. "Sorry, I don't have a clue." He had started to replace the bill on the coffee table when his blue eyes blazed and he jerked his hand and the bill back. "'Alf a mo'!" The scratchy voice was triumphant. "I do know. Up at North End a new 'otel's goin' up, an' they're blastin' out a small anchorage for private boats. I saw a blinkin' charge go off meself day before yesterday."

"The hundred's yours."

He tossed me his truck keys. His expression was absent-minded; his attention was fixed on the bills still on the coffee table as though wondering how he might increase them. "If you need a partner to 'elp requisition the explosives, guv'nor, I'm willin' to 'ave a go at it wif yer."

I almost said yes, then changed my mind. If something went wrong and I had to get away from the hotel construction site in a hurry, I had more confidence that I could make it than that Hurricane Ronnie could. And if he were along, I'd have to look out for him. The *Matilda* was crucial to Erikson's escape, and nothing should be allowed to interfere with that. "Just meet me at 1:30. Wear dark clothing and shoes, not sandals. And get some kind of knit pull-over cap to cover all that hair."

"Whatever you say, guv'nor." He gave a wave of his hand that included all three of us, and Chen Yi took him to the door.

"I like him," Hazel declared. "I think he'll do all right."

"I hope so," I said as Chen Yi returned to the Incense Room. "Speaking of clothing, does Candy have any work clothes here?"

"A closetfull," Chen Yi said. "He works two or three days as a mason every once in a while so he can show a means of support if he's questioned about it. I'll show you."

She took us to a bedroom that was the twin of the one Hazel and I were occupying and opened the closet door. I pulled out cement-encrusted work trousers and shirt and made a speedy changeover. The shirt was too large in the shoulders and the pants were too short in the legs, but I managed. There was a pair of concrete-laden heavy boots on the closet floor, and I kicked off my shoes and put on the boots.

On the closet shelf was a black beret. I took off my wig and handed it to Hazel, then pulled the beret on over my bald pate. Hazel giggled nervously. "Doesn't he look like an undernourished Yul Brynner?" she appealed to Chen Yi. The Chinese girl smiled sympathetically.

There were work gloves on the shelf, and I tried on a pair. When they fit, I shoved them into a back pocket. "Does Candy have a tool kit?" I asked Chen Yi.

"Not unless it's in the kitchen drawer next to the stove," she answered.

I went into the kitchen and opened the drawer. Candy evidently wasn't too much of a do-it-yourself man. There were four masonry trowels in the small drawer, a large and a small screwdriver, and a ball-peen hammer. I took the two screwdrivers.

"Is it dark out yet?" I asked Chen Yi.

"Not quite."

We wandered back into the Incense Room. I sat down on a divan after placing a towel on it to protect it from the work clothes. Nobody seemed to have anything to say. Hazel had a look on her face which indicated that things were moving faster than she had anticipated.

After awhile I got up and pulled one of the window draperies aside. It wasn't full dark but dark enough. "This shouldn't take too long," I said to them. Hazel didn't say anything, but she followed me to the door, where she caught my hand and squeezed it for a moment. Chen Yi came downstairs with me to let me out the door of the massage parlor which was locked.

"I know he doesn't look like much, but Candy says Cap'n Firbank has *machismo*," Chen Yi said in her soft voice.

"Let's hope he doesn't need it," I replied and went out. I walked around to the rear of the building. The truck was a panel job, an elderly Ford. The first time I started the engine it flooded, and I made a mental note to go easy on the choke.

At the end of the block I saw a car coming directly at me. A horn blew indignantly, and I remembered Nassau had left-hand-drive traffic. I pulled over and concentrated on what I was doing. I saw only a single pair of taillights ahead of me on the road to North End, and no cars came the other way. The car-driving population of the island was now at home near Oakes Field or Lyford Cay.

I had no trouble finding the hotel construction site. I drove past its steel girder framework, then turned around, and drove past it again. There was no sign of activity. I parked a quarter mile beyond it off the roadway on the wrong side by US standards. I got out of the car, traversed a ditch of soft sand, and struck out across gently rolling, gravelly terrain.

There was a moon, but it was just a sliver. Some of the stars appeared to give off more light than the moon. It was dark enough for me to stumble over low bushes until my eyes became accustomed to the absence of light. The wind was from the ocean, light and steady. It carried damp sea smells. My footsteps were cushioned in the sandy gravel.

I topped a small rise and came in sight of the construction area. It was surrounded by poles about twelve feet high between which were strung strands of wire furnishing power to regularly spaced, bare light bulbs. The illumination was obviously designed to discourage trespassers and to assist a night watchman in the completion of his rounds.

I hunched down next to a low scrub oak and waited. Ten minutes went by before a man rounded the corner of the first floor construction about twenty yards from me. He was stoop shouldered and had on a light blue windbreaker and dark trousers. I looked at my watch, then settled down to await his next circuit.

I felt cramped in every muscle by the time he appeared again. My watch said that thirty-five minutes had elapsed. I crept forward a little and settled myself behind a fifty-five-gallon steel drum. I needed to know if the watchman's thirty-five-minute circuit was his regular one.

The night breeze grew chilly while I waited. I was glad for the heavy work clothes. My watch ticked off thirty-two minutes before the watchman showed up again. I had verified his circuit time, and more important, he didn't seem to have a dog with him on the site. Moreover, from the quick glimpses I'd had of him the watchman didn't seem to be young or particularly alert.

I had studied the layout while clocking the watchman. I could see from my position a huge pyramid of sand, a thirty-foot-long stack of cement sacks piled four deep and head high, covered with protective plastic sheeting, and a huge concrete mixing machine. Beyond that lay a great bundle of steel reinforcing rods. A short distance away was a mobile trailer that probably served as the construction engineer's office. Off to one side, herded to itself by the sand pile, was a bare-board shed which I was sure was my goal.

I pulled on my gloves and resettled the beret firmly on my head. Then I ran toward the shed, keeping in the shadows of the sand pile, the cement sacks, and the concrete mixer. It was heavy going in the loose, shifting sand but almost noiseless.

The shed door was padlocked when I reached it. One glance was enough to confirm that the padlock was more of the type to discourage kids than to afford real protection. I could have picked up any of the four-foot sections of reinforcing steel rods on the ground and used it as a crowbar to snap the padlock open, but that would have made too much noise.

I took the larger screwdriver of Candy's pair I'd brought along, removed the screws from the hinge of the padlock, and lifted hinge and padlock away from the door. I opened the door carefully to avoid squeaks and stepped into the dark interior. I raised my hand above my head and swept it in a large circle. My hand encountered a light bulb hung from a pair of wires, and I pulled the chain light switch.

The shed interior jumped into focus. I didn't know if the jerry-built affair was lightproof or not, so I had to work fast. A slash-board counter supported rows of heavy tools, and underneath it were wooden boxes. The top one was open, displaying greasy-looking sticks of dynamite.

I had already taken a step in that direction when I saw the burning bar. Beside it was an oxygen tank, and I didn't even have to weigh the choice. A burning bar is a 6-foot long, inch-and-a-half-in-diameter pipe with special incendiary packing. When used with pure oxygen under pressure, it produces a flame of fantastic temperature. A burning bar will slice through feet of reinforced concrete as easily as lightning passes through copper wire. Such a tool would be quicker, quieter, and safer than dynamite.

But not lighter.

It would take more time and effort to get the equipment to the road, but I felt it was worth it. I turned off the light and went to work. I muscled the oxygen tank up into my arms and carried it outside. I set it down while I closed the door of the shed. The tank was really heavy. I alternately lugged and dragged it across the yielding sand and left it in the ditch beside the truck. My mouth was dry, my breathing was heavy, and my body was soaked with perspiration under the heavy work clothes. Candy's boots were half-filled with loose sand and felt like lead weights on my feet.

I was still gasping for breath when I reached the shed again. Inside I picked up the bar, much lighter since it was only a hollow metal tube, and turned to leave. I hadn't turned on the light the second time because I knew where the bar was, but the darkness was split by a flashlight beam that caught me full in the face. "W'at you do here, hah?" a suspicious voice said harshly.

I couldn't see the man behind the flashlight, but I could see a hand in a light blue windbreaker sleeve holding a four-foot section of half-inch reinforcing rod. This time the watchman had shaved ten minutes on his round. When I didn't answer, the steel rod moved up and then down in an arc aimed at my head.

There was no time to draw my gun. Instinctively, I

countered with the burning bar in my hands. The rod hit the bar, slid off, and came down like a whip across my left shoulder. I could hear my own grunt of pain as I staggered against the door frame. The flashlight had shifted, and I couldn't see the steel rod, but I knew it must be on the way again. I swung the bar sideways in desperation and felt it hit something solid.

Flashlight, steel rod, and watchman hit the floor of the shed with three separate, identifiable thuds. The flashlight didn't go out even after its jarring fall, and in its beam I could see the watchman's face on the floor. He was out cold. I balanced myself precariously against the door frame, dizzy with pain, trying to keep from blacking out.

Finally I made myself move. I jerked the unconscious watchman out of his jacket, which I ripped into strips. I tied his hands in back of him, tied his ankles, and then tied his hands to his ankles in back of him. He wouldn't be going anywhere for awhile. The flashlight beam was aimed at a lightweight hand truck that was probably the best method of transportation for the oxygen tank anywhere except in the surrounding loose sand.

I picked up the burning bar again and took hold of one of the twin handles of the hand truck. I dragged the whole business out to the roadside and the truck. Before opening the truck's back doors, I swung my left arm in circles to prevent the shoulder from tightening up. It wasn't only my recent labor that had my forehead beaded with sweat.

I loaded the loot into the truck. The oxygen tank almost did me in when its weight pulled at my left shoulder. No cars came along the road during the loading process. I climbed under the wheel again and headed for Candy's apartment, driving with my right hand, remembering to stay on the left hand side of the road.

I parked in the rear of the building and walked around front to the massage parlor entrance. I didn't have to knock; Chen Yi opened the door. Hazel was right behind her. "You were gone so long," she said anxiously. "Did—" She interrupted herself when she saw my face. "What happened?"

"I've got everything I need," I said.

Chen Yi's eyes were upon me as I moved inside. "What is the matter with your shoulder?" she asked.

"I scuffed it up getting the material. Run upstairs and call Hurricane Ronnie and tell him we go tonight."

The Chinese girl approached me and ran her hands lightly over my sore shoulder. Despite the delicacy of her touch I couldn't avoid flinching when she reached the throbbing tender spot. "I think it's more than that," she declared. "Take your shirt off and stretch out on one of my tables, and I will see what I can do for it when I return." She disappeared through the door leading upstairs to the apartment.

"It's not necessary," I protested to Hazel.

"You do what she says," Hazel scolded me. "Here, let me unbutton your shirt."

I was still fending Hazel off when Chen Yi returned. "He will be there as agreed upon," she said.

"That's the best news I've had tonight," I sighed.

"Take your shirt off," Chen Yi directed.

"It won't really be lame until tomorrow," I told her. "It's just stiffening a bit now."

"You may need every possible bit of freedom of movement tonight," the Chinese girl said gravely.

"She's right," Hazel chimed in.

They advanced upon me in tandem. Together they relieved me of shirt, holster, and undershirt, then stood by while I climbed onto one of Chen Yi's massage tables. Naked to the waist I stretched out on my back while she worked liniment of some kind onto her hands and then spread it onto my shoulder and upper arm and began working it deep beneath the surface.

At first it hurt like hell, but then a soothing warmth

began to spread through the shoulder. Hazel was standing on the other side of the table from Chen Yi. "Don't you think you should postpone the attempt until tomorrow night?" she asked.

"No," I said. The tied-up watchman was added inducement not to postpone the job for another twenty-four hours. And I've found when the critical point in a project is reached, postponement always seems to be the start of an unraveling process in even the best-laid plans. "I'll go while I've got the momentum." A chill little breeze started at my beltline and ran up my back. "Do you have a window open in here?" I asked Chen Yi.

"No," she said. Her strong, skillful fingers were probing ever more deeply into flesh and tissue. "Does the shoulder feel better? You are really going to have a livid bruise."

"It feels a lot better," I said truthfully. "My only concern now is about the seagoing end of the expedition."

"You can depend upon Hurricane Ronnie," Chen Yi said tranquilly. "When he says he will tie up at pier nine next to the oil company wharf at 1:30 tonight, he will be there."

Hazel looked fidgety standing there. "How about making me a cup of coffee?" I asked. I wanted to give her something to do.

"Right away," she said. She walked around the massage table and passed through the curtain hanging over the booth entrance. There was the sound of a collision and a breathless squeal. Two voices spoke simultaneously.

"Oh, I'm terribly sorry!" Hazel exclaimed.

"I'm here for my regular massage," the other feminine voice said huskily, "but if Chen Yi is busy—"

The curtain was parted again.

Flaxen blond hair surrounding a beautiful face with an English, schoolgirl complexion was thrust into the booth. Two bright blue eyes examined me curiously in the instant before Chen Yi flung a sheet over me.

"Oh, you're busy," the newcomer said. "I'll come back later."

The curtain fell again.

I felt paralyzed. The beautiful face belonged to Hermione, my erstwhile partner that first brandy-fogged night at Candy's.

Hermione, who intimately knew my chest scars, which she had just seen again.

Hermione, who had turned Candy in to her syndicate boy friend, resulting in Candy's hospitalization.

Hermione, who could be expected to do no less for me.

Hermione, who had just overheard that I would be rendezvousing with Hurricane Ronnie on pier nine at 1:30 A.M. tonight.

TEN

I BOLTED from the table with a lunge that set my shoulder to throbbing all over again. "Stop her, Hazel!" I shouted at the same instant I heard a slamming door.

I burst through the booth doorway and ran into Chen Yi standing just beyond the concealing curtain. Hazel was at the front door, peering up the street. "She's gone," she said. "Was it important? I don't see her. Should I go after her?"

"It will do no good," Chen Yi said. "Her boy friend lives somewhere near here." Her tone was bitter. "Why didn't I remember that Candy had given her a key?"

"Never mind," I said, struggling into my undershirt. "We just move up the timing of the operation, that's all. Chen Yi, run upstairs and get word to Hurricane Ronnie to get started now."

"Do you think Hermione overheard about the boat?" Chen Yi asked quietly, already on her way to the door leading upstairs.

"We won't worry about it." Chen Yi disappeared. I hoped my voice carried conviction. I wasn't feeling too confident at the moment.

Hazel closed the massage parlor front door and came over to me. "What will you do now, Earl?"

"What I planned to do, except we'll move it up two hours." I couldn't leave Hazel and Chen Yi here by themselves now that Hermione was sure to start syndicate henchmen moving in the direction of Candy's place. "Tell Chen Yi I said you should both change into something warm. We'll all be leaving here together." One of the very minor problems confronting me afterward would be what to do with Chen Yi.

"But will you be able to—"

"Move!" I blazed at Hazel. "If Hermione's boy friend lives close by, we haven't much time!" Hazel trotted through the doorway which led to the upstairs apartment.

I was three-quarters of the way into Candy's work clothes again when I realized I didn't want them. Hermione could describe them for one thing. And for the job at the back of the jail I had something better upstairs, the black sports outfit Hazel had purchased for me in Miami.

I drew my .38 and checked its action a couple of times. Then I removed the beret and work gloves from pockets of the work clothes before pulling the clothes off. I bundled everything under my arm and carried it up the stairway. I really had to lean on the bell before Hazel opened the door. "Chen Yi can't get hold of Hurricane Ronnie at the marina," she said.

"Tell her to stop trying and get dressed," I said. "It's not important." I tried to say it as though I believed it. "We'll just have to kill a little time until he shows up."

I went into our bedroom and opened dresser drawers until I found the black sportshirt and slacks. I strapped on my shoulder holster over the sportshirt, then did a couple of deep knee bends to make sure there was no binding. I was ready to go when Hazel and Chen Yi entered the bedroom. Both were dressed in dark, snugly fitting trousers and high-necked coolie jackets of quilted material secured down the front by decorative frogs. I was pleased to see that both wore shoulderbags which left their hands and arms free.

Hazel had her hair skinned tightly to her head, held in place by a silk scarf knotted into a headband. Chen Yi had on some kind of form-fitting, wrap-around headgear that contained her long black hair. Both wore flat, thick-soled Chinese slippers that enabled them to move almost noiselessly. They looked villainous enough to be Chinese river pirates.

Chen Yi removed a dark green windbreaker from her arm and handed it to me. "Put on this jacket of Candy's," she said. "It will be chilly on the water."

If we make the water, I thought to myself, but I took the jacket. "You two go downstairs and around to the back and get the truck started," I said, handing Hazel the keys. "Don't use too much choke. I'll be right there."

They left the bedroom. I slipped into the windbreaker and zipped it up. Then I experimented with high and low zipper levels while I practiced drawing the .38 until I was sure I had complete freedom of movement.

When I was satisfied, I stuffed the work gloves into a hip pocket, pulled on the beret again, and started downstairs after the women. Two-thirds of the way down to the ground floor level, I froze. A harsh masculine voice was yelling something inside the massage parlor. I drew the .38 again and crept down the remainder of the stairway and tiptoed to the open door.

Hazel and Chen Yi were standing slightly apart, each confronted by a man. Both men held guns. "Hell, this one's a broad, too," the man in front of Hazel was saying disgustedly. He was a stocky type with dark jowls. "What do we do now, Leo?"

"Where is he?" the dapperly dressed Leo snarled menacingly at Chen Yi. Both men had on white Panama hats. Hazel was closest to me and in my line of fire. I knew that anything less than an outright kill and these two would cut down on the two women. "All right, Cisco," Leo continued when Chen Yi remained silent. "Give this one about three raps in the teeth with the butt of your gun."

The stocky Cisco started past Hazel toward Chen Yi,

his right arm already drawing back. I saw Hazel's right hand snake into her opened shoulderbag and emerge swathed in a handkerchief, and I knew what was coming. The unsuspecting Cisco walked right into Hazel's round-house swing.

She unloaded the roll of nickels in her clenched fist alongside his jaw so hard his hat popped off his head. He lurched into a silly, sideways stagger as his gun clattered to the floor. He hit the wall and caromed from it, then slid to the floor and sprawled there unconscious.

Leo had turned his head at the sound of the SPLAAAAT! of Hazel's wallop landing. Before I could move, Chen Yi had clamped both hands on the dapper gunman and swung him clear of the floor completely above her head. She had discarded her slippers and was barefoot. Leo yelled hoarsely as Chen Yi slammed him down so violently that he bounced. His white hat rolled away. Chen Yi leaned down and slapped the gun from his limp hand, kicked him in the throat, then stamped twice on his Adam's apple with her heel, crushing it beneath her weight.

It all happened so fast one of the white hats was still rolling on the floor when I came out of my trance and sprinted into the room. Hazel was blowing on her knuckles. Chen Yi was stepping into her slippers again. "You two kind of make a guy feel like a fifth wheel," I said, trying to lighten the atmosphere.

I ripped down a cubicle curtain and tore it into strips to serve as tie cords. If I'd been alone, I'd have put a bullet into each man on the floor, but I couldn't see the women doing life for a murder rap if we didn't make it all the way. I tossed the strips to Hazel, and she knelt quickly and began tying up her victim as deftly as a calf roped for branding.

"You will not need to tie this one," Chen Yi said. She wasn't even breathing hard. There was a strong note of satisfaction in her voice. "He was the worst in what they did to Candy."

A closer look at Leo indicated what she meant. The least that had happened to that formerly dapper individual under Chen Yi's lethal footwork was a badly damaged larynx and voice box. He wouldn't be making a sound for a long time, if ever.

I gagged Cisco with a strip of curtain material, then herded the women outside. The syndicate rat pack was sure to have reinforcements on the way. We rounded the building and crowded into the truck's front seat. "What will you do now?" Hazel asked in a hushed voice.

"What I planned," I repeated. Psychologically, once an operation is initiated, its outcome should never be questioned. Lay it out and follow it through is the basic rule. Improvise only when you find a need for it.

The panel truck started up with a jerk as I headed for Cartwright Street. This time I remembered to keep to the left-hand lane. The equipment in the back of the truck began to rattle as we hit a few potholes in the side streets I drove on to avoid the main intersections.

Hazel twisted around in the front seat to peer into the body of the paneled rear. "What's that thing that looks like a length of steel tubing?" she wanted to know.

"That's a burning bar. It's what will spring Karl." There was a dull thud as the heavy oxygen tank hit the floor of the truck after a bounce. "And that's a tank of oxygen to fire up the bar."

"A left turn here will eliminate a main street," Chen Yi interposed. Her voice was composed. The Chinese girl had a lot of mustard in her system.

I turned left, then nudged Hazel with my elbow. "The bar and the tank make it a two-man job, kid, so buckle up your girdle. You'll be the second man. After we get rolling and I tell you to do something, you do it like five minutes ago, catch?"

"I catch." There was a moment's silence in the swaying truck. "You sound awfully confident."

"I am."

And I was at least about getting Karl Erikson out of his cell. The walls of the building holding him would be about as effective as papier-mâché against the assault of the burning bar. After that I wasn't nearly as confident. Since I'd had to move the operation up, there was a knotty question about where we were going to spend our time until the *Matilda* showed up and I was able to slip Erikson aboard.

I switched off the lights of the truck as we turned into Cartwright, and I located the alley. I tried to remember how far along it the loose board in the fence had been, then braked to a stop. We all climbed out into the alley's pitch blackness.

Hazel and Chen Yi waited at the rear of the truck while I trailed my hand along the fence in search of the loose board. It was farther away than I expected, but when I found it, I wrenched it free as rusty nails squealed shrilly, a heart-stopping sound in the stillness.

I tried the opening to make sure I could actually get through the gap. There was no problem. I returned to the women at the rear of the truck. "Chen Yi, after we unload the stuff, you move off in the truck and circle the block. Do it slowly. Keep your lights off in the alley and keep looking for Hazel. She'll come through the hole in the fence first and my partner and I will follow in a couple of minutes. If we don't show in that length of time, you two take off. No waiting, understand? You keep circling with the truck until Hazel comes back through the hole in the fence. Got it?"

She nodded, and I squeezed her arm. I caught a flash of her white teeth as she smiled. I opened the truck doors, hauled out the burning bar, and handed it to Hazel. I muscled the oxygen tank to the ground with a reminding twinge from my shoulder. It hit the alley dirt with a dull clank, but it didn't bother me. At a certain point in any operation a little boldness affords its own concealment.

I disregarded the hand truck. Speed was important now, and I didn't want to take the time to work it through the hole in the fence and drag the oxygen tank to it. "Follow me," I said to Hazel. I took a deep breath, muscled the tank up into my arms, inched my way sideways through the fence gap, and trotted to the back of the building wall. I could hear Hazel right behind me lugging the burning bar. I could also hear the diminishing sound of the truck's engine as Chen Yi drove out of the alley.

My shoulder felt like an aching tooth, and I was panting heavily when I set the tank down against the building wall, then lowered it until it was flat on the ground. There was no sound from inside. Only a single faint light showed from the left hand end of the building. I counted windows until I located the one where I'd seen Erikson that afternoon. "Climb up—when I make a leg—and see if you—can see him," I whispered to Hazel between rasping breaths.

I leaned bent kneed with my back supported by the dried-brick wall. Hazel climbed up on my knee cap platform. I'd barely locked my hands around the back of her leg to steady her when she dropped to the ground. "I saw him," she breathed against my ear. "But there's another man in there with him. I didn't see any guards."

"Some goddamn drunk thrown in with him who'll get underfoot," I said in disgust. "Well, the hell with it. Squat down here." I sat her astraddle the oxygen tank. "We could have used a little practice with this, but listen closely to me now."

I tapped the top of the tank. "See this hose and handle attachment?" I continued. "That's the pressure control valve that meters the flow of oxygen into the bar. The hose attaches to the base of the bar—" I screwed the coupling together as I spoke "—and feeds oxygen through the bar's hollow center to its ignited muzzle. The oxygen powers burning thermite which produces a flame about seven degrees cooler than a reactor pile."

"What controls it?" Hazel whispered.

"You do." I placed her hand on the oxygen flow control knob. "The higher the pressure, the hotter and more concentrated the flame becomes. It's really just a variable-length torch but with nearly the heat capacity of a solar flare."

I thought back over the procedure in my mind to be sure I'd covered everything. "When I say 'Now!,' you turn the knob and feed the bar a steadily increasing supply of oxygen. And when I say 'Go!,' you turn loose of everything and get the hell out through the hole in the fence. We'll be right behind you. All set?"

"Yes." I could hear the tension in her voice.

"Relax, baby," I told her. "This is the number on the wheel we came here to play."

The tank's high pressure hose and the length of the burning bar brought me to within six inches of the wall. Much too close. I backed off while I carefully unscrewed the threaded cap that covered the business end of the bar. In the darkness I couldn't see the greasy substance smeared around its muzzle, but the strong odor of its chemical compound assailed my nostrils.

I glanced upward to make sure I was directly beneath Erikson's window, pulled on my work gloves, then worked my hands backward until they were almost half the length of the bar away from the torch end. "Now!" I said. I heard the faint hiss of oxygen as Hazel turned the knob that opened the valve to permit the oxygen to flow through the tube. The grease at the torch end of the bar began to smoke and stink unpleasantly; chemical reaction had been initiated, the forerunner of combustion.

In two seconds a licking blue flame surrounded the tip of the bar. The flame changed to a dull red, then to a bright orange. Finally with a faint sputtering sound the entire rim of the tube burst into an intensely white phosphorus glare.

The white flame stretched out to a foot in length. It looked like a chopped-off spray of sunlit water coming from a garden hose. The hissing sound had built up to a low roar. When the flame was two feet in length and no larger than the tube's diameter, I took a long breath. "Go!" I called. Hazel slithered from the tank and disappeared outside the shallow perimeter of phosphorus light.

I directed the dragon tongue of flame beneath the window, close to the ground. I made a circular sweep of the roaring torrent of flame, and immediately, bits of charred brick and plaster exploded and burst away from the superheated wall. Steam and smoke marked the course of the torch cutting its way through brick, lathing, stone, and the plaster and paint of the interior wall. "What the hell?" I heard a startled voice say from inside.

I had no mask, and I had to keep turning my face away from the heat. Hot bits of building material sprayed onto my gloves, burning my hands even through the gloves. I could smell the odor of burning cloth as sparks burnt themselves out in Candy's windbreaker. The way the burning bar was eating its way through the wall I knew I had an overkill tool in my hands. The smoke was getting thicker, and I could hear someone coughing.

The weakened wall collapsed and crumbled even before I joined the circular flame-edged slice to its point of origin. Bricks, mortar, burning ends of two-by-fours, and flickering, flame-fringed laths tumbled out into the yard.

"Shag it out of there!" I yelled.

I couldn't see the interior of the exposed cell because of the billowing smoke. The wall was burning openly. Then a figure smaller than Erikson's should have been scrambled through the hole, running doubled up to escape the flames curling at its edges. My first thought was that a drunk shouldn't be able to move that fast, and then I saw a revolver in his hand.

The smoke-blinded, doubled-up new arrival couldn't see me. I raised the burning bar again. One wrong move with the revolver and I'd liquefy him. I was so intent on the slack gun-hand that I didn't notice action behind me.

Two strong arms wrapped around me, and two big hands gripped the burning bar and directed its flame to one side. "Hold it, Earl," Karl Erikson's welcome voice said in my ear. "That chicken you're planning to fricassee is your old buddy Jock McLaren."

"Jock—!" I swallowed the rest of what I had been about to say. "Quick! Out through the hole in the fence!" I aimed the flare momentarily in that direction to give them guidance, then reached down, and turned off the oxygen valve. The white hot, hissing flame died out.

I was the last one through the fence. Erikson was hugging Hazel exuberantly. "Earl!" she exclaimed when she saw me. "Chen Yi says a car followed her each time she circled! She thinks it followed us from the apartment!" She was staring over Erikson's shoulder at McLaren. "Who's that man?" she asked in bewilderment.

"An added starter," I said. "You and Hazel and McLaren climb into the back," I said to Erikson, opening the doors at the rear of the truck.

"Goddamn it, Drake," Jock McLaren complained bitterly as they all climbed in, "all you've done is drag Karl out into the open for them to get at him! I had the wheels greased so the Bahamian government would have eased him out of here in another three weeks if you hadn't butted in!"

"And in another three weeks I'd have gone out of my skull in that cell," Erikson said flatly. "I was never so glad to see anything in my life, Earl, as your ugly puss atop that fence this afternoon."

I closed and latched the rear doors, then ran forward to

the truck's side window. "Where did you last see the car?"
I demanded of Chen Yi.

The Chinese girl jerked a thumb over her shoulder.
"At the mouth of the alley behind us. It remains always the
same distance in the rear."

"Okay," I said. "Drive to the other end of the alley and
wait. I'll be along in a minute."

The truck pulled away. Before the sound of its wheezing engine died out, I heard a new motor sound, higher
pitched and much more powerful. The dark blur of a
sedan without lights on came down the alley. I could
barely make it out even in the added illumination furnished by the flickering flames from the jail cell.

I was standing beside the hole in the fence. I stepped
back into the gap, and I had my gun in my hand. I
couldn't imagine how they could keep tabs on us so
accurately in the darkness unless they had an owl eye,
a nightscope used in Army field maneuvers. Excited,
British-accented voices sounded from the smoldering jail.

I couldn't see how many were in the sedan. I could
hardly see the sedan. I fired three shots, two at the right
front tire and one at the left. Someone shouted as the
car veered sharply into the fence. Planking flew like
popcorn, one piece grazing my shoulder. The sedan plowed
through the fence, across the sandy yard, and rammed
solidly into the jail wall with a grinding, metal-crunching
crash barely six feet from where I'd burned the hole in the
wall.

I was running up the alley while the sound of tinkling
glass was still in the air. I jerked open the truck door
on the passenger side and scrambled in beside Chen Yi.
"Take off!" I barked at her.

"What was that shooting?" McLaren demanded sus-
piciously.

I didn't answer him. The truck lurched forward and
turned the corner. I twisted around to look into the back
of the truck. "We're two hours ahead of the rendezvous

time at the dock because they rousted us at the hideout apartment and I had to move early," I said. "Anyone got any ideas where we could spend the time? If—"

"There's another car," Karl Erikson said quietly. He was crouched down on his heels on the truck bed, talking through the glassless rear window.

Chen Yi had no sooner straightened the truck out after the turn when a sedan that could have been the twin of the first one pulled away from the curb and fell in behind us. "Turn the next corner, Chen Yi," I said, "then slow down enough for me to slip out and fix their wagon."

"No!" Erikson and McLaren exclaimed as one. "It might be the police," McLaren added.

"The police would have lights and sirens, you idiot!"

"No," Erikson said again. "Not out in public like this. Someone might get hurt."

"The government conscience," I rasped. "Why don't I just have Chen Yi drive you back to Cartwright Street where you can turn yourselves in?"

"You've botched even that possibility," McClaren declared. "With this mess on top of the other we'd be lucky to be processed out in an ordinary lifetime."

"The only way I'll go back to Cartwright Street is if they carry me." Karl Erikson's voice wasn't loud, but his tone carried conviction. His hand gripped my shoulder solidly. "This crowd doesn't want any trouble in public, either, or they'd have made a move before now. What they'd like is to get us in a deserted area. Is there any chance your man might be early at the rendezvous?"

"Chen Yi?"

"It is possible, but who knows?" she replied.

"Where's the rendezvous?" Erikson asked.

"Pier nine, next to the Commonwealth Fuel and Petroleum Warehouse dock."

"It's not what you'd call public, but it's not really deserted, either," Chen Yi added.

"Drive there," Erikson directed. "We'll hope your boat-man is ahead of schedule."

Chen Yi made a left turn, and the truck clattered toward the wharves. In the side-view mirror I could see the second sedan pacing us a hundred yards to the rear.

"Why haven't we heard the police chasing us?" Hazel wondered.

"We got a break," I explained. "The sedan I derailed smashed into the back of the jail, and from the way it hit they'll be sorting out the contents for awhile. The police won't even be sure for awhile that these two weren't in it." I turned again to look into the back. "How in hell did you happen to be at Cartwright Street, Jock?"

"I was sent there to make sure Karl had protection until his release was effected. When the man clearing out the office in New York described you and said you'd been trying to leave a briefcase for Karl, I realized—"

"Where's the briefcase now, Earl?" Erikson cut in.

"At the Lambert Warehouse and Storage Company in Alexandria." I added details quickly about making up the crate and shipping it.

"I realized something must have gone wrong," McLaren resumed, "although I didn't know what Karl's latest assignment was. I called Washington and gave them the word, and ten minutes later I had orders to come to Nassau myself. Through a negotiated agreement at a bureau-to-bureau level I was to be placed in Karl's cell until the higher level diplomatic negotiations for a full release were worked out."

"And why the hell it took so long I'll never understand," Erikson said. "With Jock's documentation the release should have been automatic."

"Red tape," McLaren said. "One thing, Earl. How did you get away from the two men the office sent to Ely to recover the briefcase from you once we realized what was going on?"

"Those were *government* men?"

"Yes, what did you think?"

"I thought it was the syndicate. Hazel's early warning system told us two men were on the way, so we took off. You government types have a certain lack of communication in your operations."

"For once I'd have to agree with you," Erikson said wryly.

"That was a hell of a move you put on the back of that jail building just now," McLaren said to me with more of his usual amiability. "When I woke up inside there, I thought Dante's *Inferno* was having a rerun. I was positive it was the syndicate after Karl. We'd been expecting it, and I was—"

"We are getting close," Chen Yi interrupted in an apologetic tone of voice. The truck was weaving through a tangled complex of narrow lanes. The night air became suddenly more humid.

"D'you think the syndicate was actually smooth enough to stand in the wings while I pulled you out of the fire as the big fat chestnut they wanted?" I asked Erikson.

"No. I think they lucked into that by trailing you to the jail, and sometime you'll have to tell me how they got close enough to you to be able to do that."

"My peculiar style of beauty."

He nodded. "A bad break but—"

"Pier nine," Chen Yi announced. She braked the truck to a stop. The ancient vehicle had been making so much noise in transit that even with the motor still running it was comparatively quiet. The truck's nose was pointed directly at a narrow pier alongside a much wider pier at which a tug and barge were moored. There was no fishing smack moored at the end of the narrow pier.

"He's not here yet," I said.

"Drive out on the pier, Chen Yi," Erikson ordered. "As far as you can go."

"We're dead ending ourselves," I warned.

"We're buying time," Erikson said. "These goons behind us don't give orders, they take them. I've found the situation useful before in dealing with the syndicate. They'll make no move without instructions unless your boatman pulls in here."

The truck inched forward, rumbling slowly over wooden planking that wasn't much more than twice the width of the truck. "If the girl in the massage parlor heard everything, they know we're going out by boat," I told Erikson. "Couldn't they be using the delay to round up some water transport of their own?"

He rubbed his chin. "You're right. I'd overlooked that point." He raised his voice. "This is far enough."

The truck stopped again, two-thirds of the way out to the end of the wharf. This time Chen Yi turned the motor off. It was so quiet I could hear wavelets lapping against the piles under the pier. "Their car is sitting back where we stopped before," McLaren reported. "Nothing's happening."

"They think they have us penned in," Erikson said.

"Think, hell!" I snorted. "We are penned in unless that damn fishing boat shows up, and even then they'll be all over us like maggots on a dead cat."

"I don't think I care for your simile," McLaren said. "If—"

He stopped when Hazel reached across him to tug at Erikson's arm. She pointed to the dark outline of the tug and barge moored at the next pier a few feet closer to the end of the wharf than our position. "We could run that," she said.

"Run it?" Erikson queried.

She gestured impatiently. "Board it and take off."

"Piracy?" Erikson said. He actually sounded shocked.

"Great!" I said, and I meant it. "Forget your ex-Navy scruples and get us off this time bomb we're sitting on here."

He was looking at the tug and barge. "I'm sure the tug would be no problem, but unless we could cast off the tow, it would be a damn sticky wicket. Towing is a tricky technique."

"Get aboard and see if it's possible," I urged him. "Hazel can be your first mate. But let's turn this truck first. Crossways, so it blocks the approach to this end of the pier."

Erikson, McLaren, and I worked the truck back and forth in a series of wheel-cramping maneuvers until we had it at right angles to the pier. There was barely a foot of clearance at either end.

"They're getting out of their car," Hazel said. She had been watching the sedan at the inner end of the pier. "They've seen what we're doing."

I drew my gun which I had reloaded previously. McLaren already had his in his hand. "Get to the tug before they rush us," I told Erikson.

"They won't rush us until they have no other recourse," he said. "The recovery of the material we took from the bank is their prime interest. Killing us off wouldn't help them recover it."

"Here comes an emissary," McLaren said.

We all looked shoreward.

It was quite an emissary.

Hermione was walking hesitantly along the pier, glancing back over her shoulder occasionally, her blond hair ruffled by the night breeze but standing out even in the semidarkness. "We want to talk to you!" a male voice shouted from the sedan.

"Who's that?" Erikson wanted to know, staring at Hermione.

"They brought her along to identify me," I said. "Which she's especially able to do. I'll go talk to her."

I had taken a step forward when a palm was placed against my chest. My forward progress stopped. "I will go talk to her," Chen Yi said and walked around the rear of the truck.

"Stop her," Erikson said.

"Wait," I answered.

The two women met at approximately the halfway point. "What is it you wish to say?" Chen Yi asked. We could hear her clearly.

"Is—is that you, Chen Yi?" Hermione's voice was a mixture of fear and bravado. "You can't get away, you know. They—they want the one I saw and the blond man from the jail. They'll—they'll let the rest of you go."

"Like they let Candy go?" Chen Yi asked evenly. Her right arm rose in a sweeping arc. We could hear the thud as her bladed palm sliced into Hermione's neck. The slighter girl staggered sideways with a choked scream and toppled from the pier. She hit the water with her neck all askew and sank like a stone.

For a count of three there wasn't a breath of sound.

Then on shore a pistol cracked twice.

Chen Yi went off the pier into the water near the spot where Hermione had disappeared.

ELEVEN

I THOUGHT Chen Yi had been hit, but in a second I saw the Chinese girl swimming powerfully in our direction.

"That will bring the police!" I rapped at Erikson. "Those goons can't sit there and wait for orders now. You and Hazel board the tug and get it started!"

"But I'm not sure—"

"They're pouring out of the sedan, Karl!" McLaren called. He was crouching behind the hood of the panel truck, peering toward the shore end of the dock. He raised his revolver and sighted.

"We'll all be back on Cartwright Street lined up in adjoining cells," I needled a strangely irresolute Erikson. McLaren's gun cracked sharply as I knelt on the dock and leaned over its edge. "Swim to the tug!" I called down to Chen Yi. "To the tug!" I straightened up as she waved a hand in acknowledgment from her position almost directly beneath me. Then she disappeared among the pilings. "Get on the tug and get a line over the side and help her aboard!" I told Hazel.

"They're fanning out!" McLaren announced. He fired a shot, waited, then fired another. I could see dark figures silhouetted against the refracted light from the shore buildings, running bent over at the end of the pier.

Erikson could see them, too, and that seemed to make

up his mind. "Come on," he said to Hazel. "And let's hope we remember something about marine diesels."

I ran to join McLaren, who was hunched down beside the truck's hood. "They won't be advancing too fast now," he said. "Moving out on this pier is like crossing a thousand yards of desert with no cover. D'you have ammunition?" He held out a box to me.

"I do, but I'll take yours, too." He slapped the small, solid box into my palm. "They'll be coming up the oil company wharf in a minute, too, as soon as they think of it," I continued. "I'll cover that from the other end of the truck."

"I say!" a high pitched, indignant voice demanded. "What's all the shoot—" There was a thumping sound and the voice died out in a gurgle.

"Karl just took care of the watchman on the tug," McLaren said. He aimed carefully toward the inner end of the pier and fired again. "I doubt if I've hit anyone, but I'm keeping them on their bellies most of the time," he said, reloading.

I dropped the box of ammunition into a pocket of the windbreaker and moved quickly to the rear of the panel truck. I could hear scrambling, splashing sounds from the next wharf as Hazel helped Chen Yi hoist herself aboard the tug. "You could have been killed!" I heard Hazel's voice.

"I owed Hermione much more than that," Chen Yi responded calmly. "What can I do here?"

"Check out the mooring lines to be sure they can be cast off in a hurry. On the barge, too, if we can't throw off the towline. I'll see if Karl needs a hand in the wheelhouse."

I was watching the shore end of the oil company wharf. "There's not so many here in front of me now!" McLaren declared at the same time I saw moving figures on the next pier.

I fired twice, deliberately high, in case the watchman had

been able to sound a shore alarm and the advancing figures were oil company personnel coming to investigate. Two winking flashes of light and the thud of a bullet crashing into the truck body close to me settled that point in a hurry.

A muffled roaring sound startled me, it was so close, and then I realized that Erikson had started the tug's diesels. The sound sputtered and died momentarily, then resumed powerfully and steady. Shouts arose from the shore as the opposition began to sense our intention. McLaren and I both fired shoreward twice more to discourage impetuosity, then reloaded hurriedly.

"Karl says get aboard!" Hazel's voice drifted to us in a brief moment of inactivity. She sounded close enough to touch with her clear voice carrying in the night.

"You first," McLaren said. "Then give me the word."

I left the shelter of the truck, leaped the intervening space to the next wharf, and ran to the stern of the tug. The bow in front of the wheelhouse was a jumble of hoisting machinery and bales of rag waste. Chen Yi was standing on the low fantail of the tug, considerably below wharf level, holding up to me a limp body. "Your partner said we should leave the watchman on the pier," she informed me.

I wrenched my shoulder all over again lifting the dead weight from her upraised hands and depositing the unconscious figure on the planking. I could hear McLaren firing steadily. I jumped down onto the fantail, then ran forward to the upper level of the wheel house so I would have an unobstructed line of fire along both wharves. "Now, Jock!" I shouted.

I heard the quick pad-pad of his approach, but I couldn't see him, and I realized how much poorer vision was looking in any direction except directly shoreward.

"Welcome aboard, Horseman," Hazel's voice said from behind me. "Sorry I forgot my bos'n's pipe."

There was a grinding noise at the tug's stern. "What the hell's that?" I demanded, startled.

"Karl told me to have Chen Yi cast off on the barge, and it's drifted into us," Hazel explained. "It's a steel towline with some kind of complicated locking device we couldn't free."

"You mean we've got to drag that lumbering—"

McLaren materialized beside me. Chen Yi was right behind him, wringing sea water from her sodden, long, black hair. "Get under cover," I said to her. "Let's get up on the roof of the wheelhouse so we'll have a better firing angle," I continued to McLaren. We climbed up on the roof, using rag waste bales and hoisting machinery tubing as stepping stones.

"Hold your fire until we need it," Jock said. "No point in giving our position away until it's necessary."

Hazel had disappeared into the wheelhouse, and the roof beneath us shuddered as the diesel's propellers bit deeply into the water. A patch of open water appeared between the tug's gunwale and the wharf. "I don't like it," I said to McLaren. "That crowd should have made a better move than that to stop us."

"You think they have reinforcements on the way?"

"By water, if they have any brains. I'll be surprised if we don't end up running a sea-going gauntlet."

Hazel burst from the wheelhouse and sprinted to the stern. Her red hair had escaped the confining scarf and was flying loosely in the night breeze, which had turned much more humid. She stood in the stern, waving her arms in circles. It was a moment before I caught on to what she was doing.

"She's semaphoring Karl on slack or no slack in the towline, so he doesn't pull the stern out of this baby," McLaren said.

"Yeah, but she's exposed. Someone's—"

A gun cracked on the pier.

I saw the gun flash halfway out on the oil company dock, and as one man McLaren and I from opposite ends of the wheelhouse roof sprayed both wharves with a withering cross fire. "One good thing about this warmer breeze," McLaren said hopefully as we reloaded again. "Combined with the cooler surface water, it should create a mist which might help us to lose any pursuit."

The steel hawser connecting tug and barge shrieked mournfully from the strain against the towing bit. The tug's throbbing increased as Erikson stepped up the rpm. Hazel darted from the stern and returned to the wheelhouse. "Karl says keep an eye out to sea," she called up to us.

"Evidently the boss shares your premonition," McLaren said.

I could feel our speed increasing, although speed was a comparative word with the waddling barge behind us. The wharf slipped away completely and became part of the surrounding blackness. I could make out no further activity on the oil company dock or on pier nine. "They can't have quit that easily," I grumbled.

"Maybe they're waiting for a boat to pick them up," McLaren suggested.

"With us limited to about five knots dragging the barge, don't even think it."

The tug's running lights came on. I stared at the green starboard and red port lights, plus the masthead light, then climbed from the roof down to the wheelhouse deck level, stumbling in the poor light over various items untidily strewn in the passageway. Hazel manned the wheel while Erikson hunched over the chart table. "What's the matter?" I demanded of Erikson. "Piracy is okay, but your brass-bound Navy soul won't permit it to be lights-out piracy?"

He straightened up and glared at me. "We've already set US-Bahamian relations back fifty years. All we need is to cream one of the hundreds of small craft in these waters, and the two governments—"

"Cruiser astern!" McLaren sang out from the wheel-house roof. "Gaining rapidly!"

"How d'you suppose the two governments would recommend handling this happy occasion?" I asked Erikson. I left the wheelhouse to rejoin McLaren on the roof.

He pointed to a spot beyond the dark hulk of the barge wallowing along in the wake of the tug. "Looks to be about a twenty-footer, and she's flying."

I grunted acknowledgment when I was able to make out the bone-in-the-teeth white bow wave of the oncoming craft. "If this is what I think it is, I have a hunch we're going to be deficient in armament in this shoot-out."

McLaren didn't say anything. I watched the cruiser rapidly narrow the gap between us. I leaned over the wheelhouse roof while lining up on the cruiser with my .38.

McLaren was doing the same. "You don't suppose it could be the water arm of the Bahamian police force?" he asked.

"The police would have lights, sirens, and a bull horn going," I answered. I could make out a figure standing with braced legs on the cruiser's bow. He had a dark object in his hands, and I knew it wasn't a violin. "Watch it, Jock!"

The cruiser came flying along the starboard side of the barge. The dark figure on the bow raised the instrument cradled in his arms. Winking red-and-yellow flashes erupted from the muzzle of the machine gun while crashing, tinkling-glass sounds blended with the thudding of bullets into the tug's bow superstructure and the wheelhouse beneath us.

The tug veered sharply as though Hazel had instinctively released the wheel for an instant. It straightened at once, but the steel towing hawser slackened and dipped beneath the surface as the barge lumbered ahead on its slightly different course. "The only thing saving us is the high bow and all of the crud on deck," McLaren said. He was watching the cruiser circle in front of us, obviously preparing for a run down the port side. "The machine gunner has a bad angle shooting upward."

I moved onto the port side of the wheelhouse roof. The cruiser roared toward us, seemingly twice as fast since it was going in the opposite direction. The machine gunner withheld his fire as the cruiser turned on a seeming dime near the tug's stern and raced between tug and barge above the slackened towing hawser.

I tried to line up on the machine gunner. The vibration of the tug, the plunging of the cruiser, and the distance made it a logarithmic computation to test the seat-of-the-pants adaptability of any wing shot. The winking red-and-yellow flashes burst from the machine gun again as I snapped off four shots as fast as I could pull the trigger.

The flashes stopped. The machine gunner spun, turned sideways, then fell backward, but he held onto his weapon. I watched in disgust while the cruiser veered sharply away out of range, and someone crawled out on the bow and retrieved the machine gun. "If that damn thing had only fallen overboard, we'd have had a chance," I told McLaren.

"That was a hell of a shot," he said. "I doubt you get another chance as good. They must have seen where the shots came from. And they can rake us from end to end, firing up over that low stern." He raised his voice. "Karl, if they cross under the stern again—"

"I know," Karl Erikson's voice said from below us. He was outside the wheelhouse, and I could see that he carried something in his hand. "Let's see if we can't fix their little red wagon," he added. "Hazel, watch the flashlight in my hand." He walked to the stern of the tug and settled himself down low against the gunwale.

"Let's hope no bright lad aboard the cruiser gets the notion to pump a few tracer bullets into the barge," I said.

"Into the barge?" McLaren repeated. "What—"

"That thing is loaded with oil and lubricants, remember?"

"But it's a long towline," he said after digesting my meaning. He was staring at the steel towing hawser, which was still beneath the surface of the water.

"Long towline, hell. If that baby ignites, we'll be roasted like ants in a picnic campfire by the heat alone. Let's just hope they still want us alive."

The pursuing cruiser was momentarily out of sight behind the barge. Then I saw it flying along on our starboard side again, repeating its first run. Erikson stood up in the stern and waved his flashlight in huge circles for an instant, then dropped down behind the gunwale again. An added surge of power from the tug's engines was evidently Hazel's response to Erikson's signal.

It might have been my imagination, but it seemed to me the stars were getting paler. I couldn't see any light in the sky, but there was a feel of dawn in the breeze that seemed warmer all the time. Growing patches of mist swirled around the surface of the water.

I was trying to line up on the machine gunner again when the cruiser turned hard aport to run under our stern for the second time. I never got the shot off. I got a glimpse of the dripping towing hawser rising silently from beneath the surface as the tug's added power put additional distance between it and the barge. The cruiser's bow smashed into the hawser, and the cruiser slammed to a halt with a shivering groan of wood and metal.

The stern rose straight up into the air in slow motion as shouts and screams carried across the water and the machine gunner was catapulted off the bow along with his weapon. The cruiser was already on its way over in what would have been a complete flip when the blunt bow of the barge crashed into it. For what seemed like minutes afterward there was the grinding sound of macerated wood and metal beneath the barge's keel.

McLaren and I dropped down from the wheelhouse roof and ran to join Erikson at the stern. "Keep a lookout," he said. "I'll get back to the wheelhouse, and we'll circle around and make sure there are no survivors."

It took us ten minutes to complete the lumbering circle and pass alongside the crumpled remains of the cruiser, which looked like wet cardboard.

There were no survivors.

TWELVE

I DON'T know how long it took us to reach Eleuthera.

Erikson and Hazel spelled each other at the wheel while the rest of us slumped on rag waste bales in attempted relaxation. Both Erikson and Hazel steered us into every patch of mist and every fog bank en route. At every movement inside the wheelhouse broken glass crunched underfoot.

Reaction had set in, and no one had much to say. Erikson spent his time during the intervals Hazel was at the wheel on the tug's radio trying to raise the Miami marine operator. It took him quite a while, but he finally succeeded. When I heard him ask for a Washington phone number, I dragged myself from my waste bale and entered the wheelhouse.

"Are you going to be able to put a lid on this?" I asked.

"No problem," he said confidently.

I pointed at Chen Yi dozing with her back propped against a bale. There were tired lines on her beautiful face. "She and her boy friend can't go back."

"Why not?" Erikson wanted to know. "We just made sure there were no survivors to report their involvement."

"We left two back at the massage parlor," I explained. "One with a crushed throat, but there's nothing the matter with the other one's voice. Even in custody he'll get to talk to the syndicate's lawyer."

Erikson nodded. "I'll take care of it. Since you obviously couldn't have managed without them, Uncle Sam will see to it that they don't suffer from the dislocation."

"Can you talk openly to Washington like this?"

"It won't be openly. When I get through to them, I'll have the duty officer set up a one-way scrambler circuit which will make us half-safe. And if anyone understands what I'm saying from this end, he'll qualify for solving code ciphers."

I went back outside.

Almost another hour went by before Erikson called to me. "What was the order number on the crate containing the material that you shipped?" he asked when I went into the wheelhouse again.

I knew it by heart, but I took the slip of paper from my wallet and showed him where I'd written it down. "GSA1234510," I said.

He transmitted it as letters of the alphabet and not consecutive letters. "Size and descriptive identification?" he asked.

I gave it to him as closely as I could remember. I held up a hand when he seemed to be nearing the end of his conversation. "Chen Yi's boy friend, Candy Kane, is still in a hospital in Nassau," I said.

"Send her in here, and I'll take care of the details of moving him out right now," Erikson replied. I went outside and roused the Chinese girl and sent her in to talk to Karl. She emerged in a few moments, smiling.

Karl Erikson was also smiling when he walked out onto the deck. "What now?" I asked him.

"We'll have a police cruiser escorting us into an unused pier at Eleuthera."

"Police!"

"No cells this time," he assured me, his smile widening. "We'll be guests but only until some special transportation is laid on. A few hot lines are glowing now between Washington and Nassau. Our favorite uncle has enough *quid pro quos* going for him in this area that we'll be ushered out with no questions asked."

"And then?"

"I've been instructed to tell you and Hazel to get lost for a month at Uncle's expense. I have to go to Washington to make the formal report, but then I'll do the same. Likewise Chen Yi and Candy. Suppose we leave it that I'll meet you two at the ranch in a month to wrap up any possible loose ends?"

I swallowed the rejoinder on the tip of my tongue to the effect that I wasn't overjoyed at the possibility of seeing him again that soon.

"Hazel tells me you bought her a twin-engine, six-passenger, two-hundred-fifty-mile-an-hour airplane," Erikson continued. "Would it do any good for me to ask where you got the money?"

"It would not."

His smile resembled that of a cat taking a dead bead on a canary. "We might find that airplane handy when she gets her ticket."

I raised my voice so that Hazel could hear me where she stood at the wheel. "Tell the lady for me that she talks too much, will you?"

My redheaded broncobuster smiled and waved at me.

Chen Yi stepped up to me when I left the wheelhouse. "A fairy tale come true," she said soberly.

"Nothing to it, baby," I assured her airily. "You tell Candy for me when you see him that I'm sorry he got his black ass fussed up, but the man in there—"I gestured toward the wheelhouse"—is going to straighten out everything. You can do your masseusing anywhere, can't you?"

"Yes. And Candy can do his gambling." She smiled, easing the tired lines on her striking features. "Thank you."

"Thank *you*," I returned. I thought about it for a minute. "You're the one who made it possible."

Still smiling, she pointed over my shoulder.

I turned to see a dark land mass rising from the water that—knowing Erikson's navigational talent—could only be Eleuthera.

Angling toward us was a low-slung white speedboat that —knowing Erikson's talent for manipulation—could only be the water arm of the Bahamian police force.

"Another day, another dollar," Jock McLaren said from beside me. He too was watching the approaching speedboat. He yawned and stretched in luxurious abandon.

I didn't answer him.

Dollar or not, after the events of the previous night it was a damned fine day to be alive.